BOUND BY THE UNBORN BABY

BOUND BY THE UNBORN BABY

BY
BELLA BUCANNON

First published in Great Britain 2016
By Mills & Boon, an imprint of HarperCollins*Publishers*
1 London Bridge Street, London, SE1 9GF

Large Print edition 2016

© 2016 Harriet Nichola Jarvis

ISBN: 978-0-263-26260-5

Our policy is to use papers that are natural, renewable and recyclable products and made from wood grown in sustainable forests. The logging and manufacturing processes conform to the legal environmental regulations of the country of origin.

Printed and bound in Great Britain
by CPI Antony Rowe, Chippenham, Wiltshire

Deepest thanks to my husband and soulmate, who claims that inside my head is the scariest place on earth but loves me unconditionally anyway. Special thanks to the generous, supportive South Australian Romance Authors for their encouragement and steadfast belief in me. And to Flo Nicoll, who saw beyond my raw writing and gave me the courage to drastically cut and revise and produce a story worth telling.

CHAPTER ONE

THIRD DOOR ON the left. Why the hell hadn't he given in to his original instinct, phoned the hotel with a refusal, then binned the short letter hand-delivered to his office? He'd never heard of Alina Fletcher—didn't have the time or energy for enigmatic invitations.

Except one phrase, vaguely referring to his family, had captured his interest five weeks after his sister and brother-in-law had died in Barcelona, less than two since his second trip to Spain regarding their estate.

He felt drained. Flying overseas and coping with local authorities while handling the glitches regarding his latest hotel acquisition had been exhausting. The basic Spanish he'd acquired on other trips had helped; deprivation of sleep didn't. He desperately needed a break to enable him to grieve for Louise, and for Leon, who'd been his best friend since primary school. Any additional angst was definitely unwelcome.

The open doorway allowed him a clear view of the woman facing the window. Slim build. Medium height. Short dark brown hair. His gaze slid rapidly over a sky-blue jacket and trousers to flat shoes. Unusual in this time of killer heels.

'Ms Fletcher?' He was curter than he'd intended, influenced by a hard clench low in his abdomen.

She turned slowly and his battered emotions were rocked even more. Pain-filled eyes underlined with dark smudges met his. Widened. Shuttered. Reopened, clear and steady. Whatever had flickered in their incredible violet depths had banished his lethargy. His dormant libido kicked in, tightening his stomach muscles, accelerating his pulse.

Inappropriate. Inexcusable.

'Ethan James? Thank you for agreeing to meet me.'

No welcoming smile. Did he detect a slight accent? He'd have to hear more—wanted to hear more.

He cleared his throat. 'Did I have a choice?' Moving forward with extended hand, he frowned at her hesitation. *She* was the one who'd requested the meeting.

After a cool, brief touch she gestured to the seating. 'Coffee? Black and strong?'

His eyes narrowed at her assumption of his preference, flicked to the wedding ring she wore. Married. Why did he care? The perfume she wore didn't suit her. Too strong. Too exotic. He wasn't thinking clearly—hadn't been since that devastating early-morning phone call.

'What do you want?' No games. Either she told him the reason they were here or he walked. 'You've got two minutes to convince me to stay.'

She met his glare unwaveringly. 'Then you'd better start reading.' Perching on the front of an armchair, she pushed a buff-coloured folder along the low table before pouring coffee into a cup.

His muscles tensed. She appeared confident, was counting on him thinking he'd always wonder if he left without an explanation. He grudgingly picked up the unnamed folder and sat, stretching out his long legs.

Once she'd placed the drink in front of him she took a book from the bag by her side and settled into the chair to read.

He pulled the file out, glanced at the front sheet— and his already shattered world tilted beyond reality. He flipped the pages, studied the signatures.

Scowled at the seemingly composed female ignoring him. A fist of ice clamped his gut. His heart pounded. Not true. Not believable. Though the signatures were genuine. He'd seen enough of them in the last few weeks to be absolutely certain.

Why? There'd been no indication.

He reached for his coffee, drained the hot liquid in one gulp while glancing at Alina Fletcher. Not so serene on further scrutiny. The fingers on her left hand were performing a strange ritual. Starting with the littlest, they curled one by one into her palm, with her thumb folding over the top. Dancelike, the movement was repeated every few seconds.

Nervous? She damn well ought to be, hitting him with this out of the blue. He gave a derisive grunt. He'd have been blindsided however she'd informed him.

Reverting to the opening document, he meticulously perused every paragraph.

Alina automatically flicked the blurred pages of her book, her fingers trembling. Her thoughts were in turmoil. This encounter ought to have been straightforward. She'd come to Sydney, acquaint the brother with the situation, and then they'd discuss options in a businesslike fashion. Instead she'd tensed at the timbre of his formal greeting, been slow to take his hand, shaken by her quickening heartbeat.

Please, please, let it be hormonal.

The best scenario was that he'd concur with the logical solution. She'd return to Europe and they'd communicate amicably via email or phone. Living alone would be no hardship. She only shared accommodation when it was required by an employer and rarely maintained friendships, even those forged from seasonal reunions. No roots. No ties. Liking co-workers was a plus. None had been able to break through the wall staying sane had compelled her to build.

She still wasn't sure what had drawn her to Louise on their early irregular meetings. Perhaps an empathy that had enabled her to see behind the sparkling personality and glimpse the hidden sorrow? A feeling that she was a kindred spirit? Seeing the loving relationship Louise had shared with Leon? She'd often thought of them while travelling. Four months ago fate had brought them together at a critical time for Louise, a soul-searching one for her.

She'd stayed away from the funeral service in Barcelona for her own sake, needing time to decide what to do. Contacting Ethan James while he was arranging for his relatives to be transported to Australia for burial would have been insensitive. It was, however, the honourable thing to do now. In the end the only thing she believed would ensure her future peace of mind.

Until she'd looked into those cobalt eyes with their thick black lashes—so like Louise's, except dulled with sadness and fatigue. Unwarranted, almost forgotten heat sensations had flared low in her belly. Immediately squashed. *Never again.* She'd barely survived before—sometimes felt she hadn't.

During the last year she'd slowly, *so* slowly, begun to open up a little to people. Now she was caught in a different nightmare, with far-reaching consequences. It all depended on the man intently scanning the papers she'd given him.

She approved of his neatly trimmed dark hair, his long fingers with well-shaped clean nails. His no-frills attitude to her letter. Leon had described him as astute, pragmatic, and extremely non-sentimental in business. Personally reserved. The very qualities she needed right now.

She sipped her mint tea, praying her guest would agree to her suggestion. Her skin still prickled from his oh-so-fleeting touch. A hint of earthy cologne teased her nostrils every time she inhaled. Unusual and unfamiliar. Definitely not one of the brands she'd sold working in a department store in Rome last summer.

The tension in the room heightened. She looked up, encountered cold, resolute scrutiny, a grim mouth and firmly set jaw. Did he intend to dispute her claim? In October he'd have all the proof he'd require.

Ethan saw fear chase the sadness from her eyes, swiftly replaced by pseudo-cool detachment.

'You're carrying their child.' He didn't doubt the validity of the documents. They were legal, watertight contracts— somewhat alien to his carefree relatives. 'Why?'

'Three early miscarriages with no medical explanation. No trouble with conception. Surrogacy offered them a way to have a baby of their own.' She spoke precisely, as if she'd rehearsed every word.

He swore quietly, fervently. Why hadn't they told him? There'd been no hint of a problem on any of his visits. Or had he been too focused on his growing business empire to notice?

Anger at lost opportunities gnawed at him. Guilt at missing any change in Louise's demeanour flooded him. The urge to strike out was strong. Pity the only one in the firing line happened to be the messenger.

'Why the secrecy? Why *you*?' He ground the words out violently.

She didn't flinch, though faint colour tinged her cheeks. Crossing her arms, she lifted her chin. 'I offered. My choice. My reasons.'

Something in her tone warned him not to pursue the subject. Fine—he'd accept the simplified statement for now. Coming to terms with being uncle to an unborn child conceived by his dead sister and her husband, carried by a stranger, took precedence.

'When's the child due? Did they know?' A myriad of questions buzzed in his brain, making it impossible to prioritise.

'Late October. I'm nine weeks. We did a pregnancy test together.' Her lips trembled. Her gaze shifted to the wall behind him. 'They were so incredibly happy for a few days. Until that goods van smashed into them at that outdoor café.'

Her tortured eyes met his. Anguish ripped through him on hearing those mind-numbing words spoken in her tremulous voice. He knew.

He'd received the international call, read the reports. Seen photographs of the mangled wreckage.

Suddenly he craved solitude. And space. He wanted to run from this woman, escape from her predicament. Forget everything and crawl into a cave like a wounded animal to lick his wounds and recover.

Not going to happen.

He ought to stay, talk more. Get more details. How could he? She exacerbated his torment.

Jamming the file into the folder, he stood up. Alina stayed in her seat, her eyes a mixture of sorrow and perplexity, making him feel like a louse. He pulled his mobile from his inside pocket.

'I need time to take all this in. Give me your number. I'll phone you tomorrow.'

She told him, including the Spanish code. 'You can leave a message at Reception so you won't get charged international rates.'

Ethan let out a short, half-choked laugh. She appeared genuinely concerned at the thought of him paying the fees—something his company did every day. 'I can stand the cost.'

A soft blush coloured her cheeks. His gut twisted in remorse.

She rose to her feet, proudly defiant, tightly

clasping her book. 'I appreciate what a shock this is. If there'd been an easier way to tell you, I'd—'

'There wasn't. Goodbye, Ms Fletcher.' He spun round and strode out.

The tension drained from Alina's muscles, to be replaced by frightening awareness. Alien. Alarming. His aura still filled the room, surrounding her, challenging her resolve. Threatening what little stability she had.

She tried to equate this barely held together man with the sharp, on-the-ball tycoon described to her. The one who'd always managed to extricate the two friends from escapades usually instigated by the younger one. The one who'd transformed a failing local travel centre into the multimillion-dollar Starburst hotel and tourism empire.

The man she'd just watched hurriedly exit seemed to be operating on stretched nerves.

Pouring another cup of tea, she reproached herself for bringing more trauma into his life, but knew she'd had no choice. The realisation that she'd been banking on him taking charge, relieving her of all major decisions, hit home. She squeezed her eyes shut, stemming the tears. He hadn't rebuffed her completely. There was still hope.

She pictured Louise sobbing in the café the day

after the specialist had advised her that any more pregnancies might be detrimental to her health. She recalled walking her home, talking with her, learning about her society-obsessed parents' rigid attitude to social status.

Her sympathy for Leon's and Louise's plight, and her strong desire to help had been understandable; the solution that had popped into her mind had been astounding. And terrifying.

After two days of intense soul-searching she'd offered to be a surrogate. Their initial refusal had given way to grateful acceptance in light of their limited options. Over a supper of fruit, cheese and dips, washed down with local wine, they'd conceived the perfect plan. Almost foolproof. They hadn't counted on brake failure destroying their hopes in the cruellest way possible.

She stroked her stomach. *Their* baby—not hers. She was simply a cocoon. In October she'd have given birth to their son or daughter and then stepped away, allowing them to experience fully the delights and dramas of parenthood.

Ethan *must* consent to her plan. This tiny new life inside her deserved the love and happiness its new family would have shared. Ethan, rather than his parents, was her preferred choice. If they all chose not to… Well, then she'd have to confront and conquer her demons.

Gathering up her belongings, she went to her room, hoping the television would prevent her thoughts from straying to tomorrow's call. And its maker.

She was window-shopping along George Street when her phone rang late the next morning.

'Alina?'

Spoken with a slightly different emphasis, as if personal to him. Silly idea. He'd given her the impression he considered her an intrusive dilemma.

'Sorry I didn't call earlier. I've been juggling my schedule. Are you free tonight?'

'Yes. I came to Sydney for the sole purpose of meeting you.'

'And if I'd refused?' he asked brusquely.

'I'd have posted you a detailed letter with the file and caught the next available flight to Spain.'

'And wha—? No, not now. A hire car will be outside your hotel at five-thirty. I've booked a table. Goodbye, Ms Fletcher.'

He hung up, leaving her startled by his broken-off question. Understanding his scepticism, she swore to be honest—though she'd keep her past to herself unless it concerned the baby. Last night as she'd fallen asleep she'd sensed an elusive unidentifiable memory skip through her mind. Didn't want any more.

Ethan drummed his fingertips on his desk. He'd meant to ask why she wore a ring—if there was a husband or partner in the picture. He'd been distracted by her impassive replies and had accidentally activated an email from Brisbane requiring an urgent reply. Hence his regrettable abrupt ending to the call.

His back ached…his brain spun. An evening on the internet researching surrogacy had raised more questions than it had answered. It hurt that they'd gone through so much heartache alone. Why hadn't they reached out to him? Surely they'd known they mattered to him more than anything?

He'd supported Louise's marriage to Leon against his parents' wishes, happily standing as best man. He had never doubted their love for each other, had admired their courage and steadfast defiance of the demands to wait until they were older. Louise's declaration that they'd have a park wedding in front of a few friends had provoked his mother into grudging agreement. She had then proceeded to turn it into a flash affair for her own social gratification.

From what he'd seen, growing up, those two had been the exception in a world of duplicity and the façade of wedded unity. His own memories of being brushed aside, of days seeing only nannies or cooks, still rankled.

Knowing he carried the genes of two people with no apparent parental feelings had determined his future. Swearing there'd be no children, even if he married in the future, he'd resolved to be the best uncle to any nieces or nephews. Now that vow would be tested in a way he'd never imagined.

Lying awake, contemplating options, he'd finally decided on the best solution for the child and his family. It all depended on that gold ring. Alina Fletcher might not concur with his decision. She was the one who'd offered the use of her body, the one who'd travelled to Australia to meet him. The one who'd spun his world out of orbit with her revelation. She'd committed herself by contacting him.

He'd been disconcerted by his physical reaction to the stranger with the inconceivable news. An effect he blamed on fatigue, combined with his almost celibate life for months. So he'd run—hadn't stayed to find out what *she* wanted, what she expected from *him*.

He'd finally slept restlessly, risen early, and reshuffled his work diary.

Alina spotted Ethan immediately: tall, head-turningly handsome, impossible to miss among the people milling outside the luxurious hotel. His sister had been spontaneous and cheerful; her dinner companion tonight exuded an aura of deliberation and sobriety.

Blaming the prickling sensation down her spine on stress, she steeled herself as she unbuckled the seatbelt. Her door opened, giving her a view of a solid torso clad in an elegant designer suit. She was glad she'd impulsively packed her black dinner dress, bought four years ago in rural France. Rarely worn, it was simple in design, chic enough to give her confidence a boost. Loose enough to conceal any hint of her condition.

She swung her leg out and his fingers curled around her elbow, taking her weight as she alighted. Holding on longer than necessary. As it had yesterday, his touch generated tingles, radiating across her skin.

'Thank you for being so prompt.'

His deep voice sounded less dynamic. The shadows under his eyes were darker. Another too-full day after too little sleep?

Why the let-down feeling at his mundane comment? Quickly followed by a zing of pleasure when he put his arm around her to escort her through the crowd? Heat flared in places that had been winter-cold for years, shocking her into silence.

He released her the moment they entered the elevator for the short journey up to the restaurant, taken in silence. They were greeted by the maître d', who led them to a window table set apart in a far corner, secluded by greenery. Alina followed, acutely aware of the man behind her and the limited number of diners in the room. She sat, staring in awe at the North Sydney high-rises across the harbour.

'This is incredible,' she said, and sighed, turning her head to take in more. Too far. Their eyes met; warmth flooded her cheeks. He must think her so gauche. To her surprise he glanced out, then smiled at her for the first time, transforming his features, making him less forbidding.

'I guess it is. Over time you get used to the sky-line being there.'

'Not possible,' she declared vehemently. 'And it's going to get better as all the lights come on, isn't it?'

CHAPTER TWO

ETHAN'S FATIGUE LIGHTENED at her enthusiasm for something he took for granted. Her eyes gleamed, darkened to the colour of the flowers of the plant on his PA's desk.

His jaw firmed as she returned the smile from the young waiter who offered her a menu. The curt nod he gave him on accepting his was unwarranted, and instantly repented.

Her delightfully intense expression as she carefully read each item restored his good humour. She finally looked up and gestured, palm out.

'How on earth am I supposed to decide? I'm not even sure what some of them are. You choose for me.'

'The lemon sole is particularly good. Or the chef's special if you are in the mood for lamb.' His gaze dropped to her pink, unenhanced lips. Forget food—he wanted to taste *her*. She'd be sweeter than any dessert coming out of the kitchen tonight.

Her voice cut through his inapt thoughts.

'I'll bet they're all delicious. Nothing too spicy or strong-flavoured.' Putting her menu on the table, she laid her arms on top, unintentionally drawing his attention as she leant forward. 'And small portions for me, please.'

The taut fit of the material over her breasts intrigued him. Had being pregnant enlarged them? They'd been hidden under her loose jacket yesterday. Tonight they'd been the first thing he'd visually noticed when she'd stepped from the car—preceded by that perfume so not right for her.

What the hell was wrong with him? The woman opposite him wore a wedding ring and was pregnant. He tamped down his libido, concentrated on selecting their meal.

'Oh, wine...?' Alina's hands fell to her sides as a young woman carrying a bottle placed an ice bucket and stand next to their table.

'Non-alcoholic,' Ethan hastily reassured her, before addressing the waitress. 'Please allow my guest to sample it.'

She savoured the tangy fruit flavour, drank a little more, and smiled. 'It's very refreshing. Thank you.'

She gazed around while he ordered their meals. A screen of plants, plus a larger than standard space, separated them from the adjoining tables. Little chance of being seen—none of being over-heard. Had he asked for it? Or—oh, this upmarket hotel must be part of his Starburst chain.

The waitress left. Alina raised her glass, let the tangy liquid slide down her throat. Her curiosity overrode tact. 'Are these plants and extra space always here?'

He shrugged. 'On request. Some couples find the seclusion romantic. Some men aspire to an elaborate setting with privacy for a proposal.' He paused, a glint of amusement in his eyes. 'In case of rejection.'

She understood the need to keep her presence a secret. An icy shiver ran down her spine. What if he rejected *her* proposal? She had to persuade him it was best for everyone involved.

'Doesn't it invite curiosity from people who might recognise you? Who'll wonder who I am?'

'Few people dine this early. I believe you'll feel more comfortable eating here, then we'll go some-where quieter to discuss our situation.'

'You're right. Thank you.' Her gaze wandered from the silverware, the fine cut-glass, and the decorative light fittings to the amazing panorama outside the window.

'Fine dining. Romantic setting with harbour lights. They create a wonderful memory for any couple,' he commented.

Like a sandy beach with rippling waves at dawn. Her eyes misted. She bit the inside of her lip. *Don't go there. It's all gone. Gone for ever.*

Ethan wasn't about to let her attention stray. He had too much to learn in too little time. Her history. The reason she'd agreed to be a surrogate. Why she wore that ring. Why a simple piece of jewellery rankled so much.

'Alina?'

Too sharp.

She started, blinked twice, and refocused. 'I'm sorry. I was miles away.'

'I noticed.' He leant an elbow on the table, rested his chin on his hand, and scrutinised her. He sensed her superficial demeanour was a defensive shield, preventing her from revealing anything personal. It was one he aimed to breach for his, and the child's, benefit.

'Relax. Enjoy your meal. You like seafood?'

'Love it.'

Her words coincided with the appearance of their appetiser: creamy pumpkin soup with croutons. They ate in silence, apart from her praise for the country fresh flavour. He signalled for the empty dishes to be removed, requested their mains be held for five minutes.

Once they were alone, he leant forward. 'How long had you known Leon and Louise?'

'Oh. Um… I guess casually for more than three years. If there was a position vacant I worked in a café near their house whenever I was in Barcelona.'

'A waitress?' His eyebrow quirked. *Whenever she was in Barcelona? She was not a resident?*

She bristled at his inference of her pursuing a lowly profession. 'Be careful, Mr James. You're demeaning your staff, who are giving us excellent service tonight.'

He acknowledged her rebuke with a nod. She looked gratified and continued. 'It's a useful skill for a working traveller. I rarely stay anywhere for long.'

'Any other *useful* skills?' This was getting worse by the minute. Casual worker. Temporary. No profession. Why had they chosen *her*?

Alina fought the urge to challenge his condescending attitude. He was the baby's uncle—ideally its future guardian.

Her choices had been determined by her need to have limited social contact. She toyed with the stem of her glass, drew in a steadying breath. 'Any office work, translating or bar tending. Plus anything seasonal or transient, such as crop harvesting. I have references, if you're interested. It's been my life for seven years—my choice.'

'Not any more. Your foreseeable future will be governed by what's best for the child you are carrying. And I will have an input in every decision.'

His low, inflexible tone added to the challenge in his piercing eyes. She matched him, picturing his relatives' joy—so short-lived.

'The baby *is* my main priority. I'm taking care of myself, eating healthily, exercising sensibly.'

The bite in her voice shamed her. She'd never been confrontational, had always tried to get along with others, even in short-term work environments.

She gulped, tried for conciliation. 'Everything I do is to maintain their dream.'

Their dream—not hers. Talking with Ethan James raked up memories best left forgotten.

'What nationality are you? Where are your legal documents? Birth certificate?' He topped up their wine glasses as he spoke, then watched her as he drank.

Hands hidden in her lap, her spine rigid, she refused to show any sign of weakness. 'I'm Australian, born and bred. Is that good enough for you? For your parents? My passport's in the safe at the hotel.'

She'd done it again. She'd anticipated his questions, prepared herself for suspicion, even rejection. So how did he manage to wind her up so easily?

He waited. His unfathomable dark blue eyes revealed nothing. Inexplicably, she found herself wondering how those firm full lips would feel pressed against hers.

No. No. No! She let out a loud huff of air. Had to be hormonal. Couldn't be the man. It was vital for him to think the best of her.

She tried again. 'Anything not needed regularly is with my solicitor in Crow's Nest.'

'Good. Easily accessible.' He nodded, smiled as if her reply pleased him. 'Here comes our main course.'

He'd chosen grilled lemon sole served with lightly sautéed vegetables and a side salad. It was melt-in-the-mouth scrumptious—the best meal she could remember. Her tension eased as he kept the conversation neutral and light. Because he was satisfied with her answers so far?

Dessert was an unbelievably good strawberry

soufflé. She sensed his perusal as she scraped the last morsel from her dish. Didn't care. It was heavenly.

Putting down her spoon, she smiled at him. 'Mmm. Mouth-watering food. Great service. Do you eat here often?'

'I'll pass your approval on to the chef. Apart from dining here, with or without guests, I find it convenient to ring in an order and have it sent to my office or apartment.'

'They home-deliver? Like pizza?' She stared at him in amazement. He regularly ate personally delivered gourmet meals. She occasionally ordered takeaway, saved money by picking it up.

His throaty laugh skittered across her skin. 'Hey, we cater for twenty-four-hour room service. My meals travel a little further in a taxi, that's all.'

'Wow. We *so* live in different worlds.'

His eyes darkened and bored into hers. She couldn't move, couldn't look away. Her light-hearted words had shattered the mood.

Ethan pushed his empty dish aside, annoyed at her emphatic statement. She made it sound like an insurmountable division between them. Although their life in Spain might have been simpler, more casual than his ambition-driven existence, basically his core beliefs were the same as his sister's and brother-in-law's.

He'd enjoyed every moment of the regular visits he'd made to Barcelona, including the noisy, fun-filled meals lasting well into the night. There had always been friends around. So why hadn't he met *her*? Bad timing?

He drank the last of his wine, dropped his napkin on the table. 'Are you ready to leave? We'll have privacy to talk upstairs.' Where he'd be able to override any dissension to his proposition.

'Upstairs?'

Apprehension shaded the striking colour of her eyes, and a strong urge to reassure her rocked him.

'Company suite for family or friends. Leon and Louise stayed here twice; usually they came to my apartment.'

She didn't answer. He came round to hold her chair while she retrieved her bag from the floor and stood, head held high. Courageous. Beautiful.

Taking her elbow respectfully, he guided her towards a door in the side wall. The ever-alert maître d' was there before them. Ethan thanked him, adding praise for the attending staff. A moment later they sped upwards in an exclusive elevator.

* * *

They stepped out into a foyer, not the corridor Alina had envisaged. Colourful modern art complemented the light sand-coloured walls between two white doors. He used a key card to open the one on the right, gestured for her to enter.

Her remark rang true as she stared enviously at her surroundings. Different worlds nailed it. She'd cleaned rooms, never luxury suites. And for him this was the norm, his everyday existence.

Floor-to-ceiling windows afforded a spectacular view of the city on two adjoining walls. Perfectly situated to take advantage was a dark wood dining setting, with a centrepiece of bushland flora. A matching coffee table stood in front of a luxurious dark blue three-piece lounge suite, facing a wall-mounted television. Two large bright blue and red abstract paintings hung on light grey walls.

Her companion shrugged out of his jacket, tossed it onto a chair, and gestured towards a hallway. 'The bathroom is the third door along if you need it.'

He walked across to a fancy coffee machine, reaching for two mugs from the cabinet above. She watched the play of his muscles under his navy shirt, chided herself for the sudden appreciative clench low in her belly.

'If not take a seat. Tea? I assume your condition is the reason you didn't drink coffee yesterday?'

He'd noticed. Totally focused on the documents, reeling from shock, he'd still been aware of what she'd drunk. Had he mentally sized her up, judged her, as well?

'Herbal, if you have any, please.'

'No problem. Make yourself comfortable.'

So solicitous. So hospitable. Would his attitude change if they couldn't come to an agreement?

She moved to the settee, kicked off her shoes, and curled into a corner. 'Could you make it fairly weak? Just in case.'

He glanced round, his brow furrowed. 'In case of what?' His face cleared. 'Ah, having trouble with morning sickness?'

She appreciated the concern in his voice, even if it was more for the welfare of his niece or nephew than for her.

'I've been lucky so far—occasional nausea from strong aromas, nothing too bad.'

This polite, bland conversation had no reason to irritate her—however, it did. There was no one around to hear them. *Let's get on with it.*

'What else have...? Never mind.'

Ethan tamped down his curiosity regarding her history. The current situation had priority. He put the two mugs on the coffee table and sat down beside her, inadvertently too close for detachment. Close enough to smell the fragrance he'd determined to change at the earliest opportunity. Close enough to notice the faded scar almost hidden by her hair. Close enough to inadvertently touch her. He linked his fingers to prevent impulsive movement. To keep it impersonal. *Huh, she's having Louise's child. Can't get much more personal.*

Clearing his throat, he returned to basic facts. 'Has the pregnancy been confirmed medically?' A natural question to open the conversation.

She flicked a non-existent lock of hair from her forehead. A recent change of hairstyle? Cut shorter than she normally wore it?

'No. We did an early home test on February the seventh. Although it showed positive, I repeated it before booking my flight.' Her voice was clear, with no hesitation.

He nodded. 'We have an appointment at eleven-thirty next Monday with Dr Patricia Conlan—reputedly one of Sydney's leading gynaecologists. I've been assured she'll give the best care to you and our baby. She's had a cancellation, otherwise we'd have a longer wait.'

Her pupils dilated, making a stunning display of her violet irises. Her hand moved swiftly to cover her abdomen, triggering a surge of possessiveness in him, alien and disquieting. An instinctive action? Had he imagined the flicker of awareness at his deliberate use of a certain adjective?

'You need your own proof that I'm pregnant. I'll be ready.'

'Not proof. Confirmation that everything is okay.'

She sampled her tea, smiled approvingly. 'It is. Apart from mild nausea, I'm fit and healthy. What else do you want to know?'

All your secrets. She'd been in his thoughts all day, disturbing his concentration at inopportune moments. Every time he'd walked past his PA's potted plant the flowers had conjured up a picture of stunning, sorrowful violet eyes. He'd never been drawn to any woman so fast, so powerfully. Telling himself it was because she carried Louise's child didn't cut it. His body had responded to her on sight, when he'd still suspected a scam.

'I've made frequent trips to Barcelona in the last three years. I don't remember your name being mentioned. How come we didn't meet?' There'd always been noisy gatherings at his sister's, available women and obvious attempts at matchmaking. 'I flew over for a week in January. They were excited and secretive, so I'm guessing it happened around then.'

'I deliberately wasn't part of their social group. Louise and I were casual friends who'd have a chat over coffee sometimes. Occasionally Leon would join us. I'd never been to their home until the day she confided in me. Again, my choice. The embryo was implanted on the twenty-eighth—after you'd left.'

Her gaze drifted to the window, as if she were picturing something from her past. She raised her drink and swallowed. As he watched the movement of her throat his fingers itched to caress her lightly tanned skin wherever it was exposed. Wherever it wasn't.

Draining his mug, he set it down with a sharp clink.

Startled by the noise, she swung round to confront him. 'I told you I travel a lot—mostly Europe. I'm not good at socialising or small talk.'

Merely lack of practice, to be rectified by the new circles he intended to introduce her into—a world involving business dinners and networking. She'd have his support and protection as long as she stayed with him. In return he'd expect her to accompany him to various functions when a partner was invited.

He'd been completely absorbed in her during their meal. Her eyes, her lips, the graceful curve of her neck as she bent her head, even the way she used her cutlery, all fascinated him. The plain gold ring on her left hand—the only jewellery she wore—niggled at his gut.

She still hadn't mentioned a husband or partner. It had always been 'I'. His curiosity had to be satisfied prior to revealing his intentions.

He fisted his fingers on his thigh, braced himself for her reaction. Spoke as she leant over to put her mug down. 'You wear a wedding ring. And my research informs me surrogates are invariably women who have had at least one successful pregnancy.'

She sat immobilised, one arm outstretched, her face in profile.

He couldn't stop the next words forming. 'Where's your child? Your husband?'

Her mug dropped to the table's edge, broke in two. Fell to the floor. Her skin drained of colour.

Wide, tormented eyes met his. The truth hit him like a king punch to the solar plexus a split second before she replied.

'They died.'

Flat. Expressionless. Heartbreakingly poignant.

No movement. No sound. Then without warning she erupted from the settee, her desperate eyes swinging towards the door. She took one step. Ethan sprang to his feet and caught her elbow, twisting her round. Her stricken face shook him to the core. He let go.

'I didn't think. I'm sorry, Alina.'

She gulped in a deep, staggered breath that raked her body and silently walked to the hallway.

CHAPTER THREE

THEY DIED. WHY HADN'T he realised? The travelling. The solitary lifestyle. He hadn't connected the facts. Instead he'd acted like a bastard, without consideration for her feelings. An echo of his father.

Somehow he had to make amends, persuade her to stay. The child's acceptance of him depended on her conceding to his proposition. In every way. Alina the woman as much as the child-bearer. *Oh, Louise, what have you started? Why didn't you tell me?*

He picked up both mugs, dropped hers into a bin, washed his, and waited.

Alina sat on the toilet seat lid, hugging herself, rocking rhythmically, trying to quell her shuddering breaths. The cloud in her mind began to clear, leaving behind a mixture of fear and shame. She'd blown it—been ambushed by a question she ought to have foreseen. Ethan James was a man who'd check the information he'd been given—investigate until he knew everything. Or believed he did. And instead of calmly answering, she'd panicked.

She cringed, dreading what his opinion of her would be now—a neurotic female with serious hang-ups who claimed to be pregnant with his niece or nephew. It was essential he be convinced of her emotional stability, so he'd trust her to take proper care of herself and the baby until its birth.

Dampening a cloth from the rail with cold water, she pressed it to her face, ashamed of her abrupt reaction. Her reflection in the mirror was pale and strained—not the composed image she'd hoped to project. *For Louise and Leon.* She recited her mantra, squared her shoulders, and returned to the main sitting area.

Ethan leant on the counter by the coffee machine, watching her with sympathetic eyes. Guilt also flickered in the cobalt blue, stirring her conscience.

She gave an awkward shrug. 'You surprised me. I anticipated a doctor asking about my history, but I guess I'm not as prepared as I thought. Add my hormones acting crazy, and jet lag—'

'My fault. I didn't mean it to come out so brutally.' He moved forward, gave her plenty of space.

'My only excuse is I'm still trying to come to grips with it all. Forgive me?'

She empathised—had been there. Heck, she was *still* there. Shock upon shock robbed you of lucidity. In the last twenty-four hours, she'd delivered a bundle to him. Not having any option didn't ease her remorse.

She managed a twisted smile. 'Time heals is a furphy. Developing a façade to get through each day is the only way to survive.' And hers threatened to crack with every look, every touch from this man. Her mouth dried; her throat constricted. 'It's not right. They deserved to have their baby. Life *stinks*.'

Fierce and heartfelt.

Ethan concurred that life wasn't always fair, but refrained from admitting it. 'Life's what you make it. Are you up for talking a little longer? If not I'll take you to your hotel and we can continue in the morning.'

'I'll stay.' She ran her tongue over dry lips. 'Could I have another tea, please?'

'Thank you for agreeing. Same flavour?'

With a brave attempt at smiling, she curled into the corner of the settee. When he sat he left a bigger gap between them, avoiding accidental contact.

Space didn't help. Yesterday he'd attributed his reaction to her as the combined effects of disbelief, weariness, and self-enforced celibacy due to his business commitments. Problems with the expansion of his hotel chain into Queensland—on top of his regular heavy workload—had left him little time for a personal life even prior to the accident.

Tonight the desire for physical contact had been—*was still*—much stronger. He'd resisted with effort, knowing it was essential to allay her doubts and resolve some of the essential matters. Every day counted in the agenda he'd formulated.

She drank thirstily, colour gradually returning to her cheeks. Unsure eyes met his and he thought he'd have given almost anything to appease her by bringing the evening to an end.

'That was the reason you kept moving? No ties? No commitments?'

Relief washed over him when she merely nodded before placing her mug down carefully.

'We need to discuss certain issues—the main one being protection for the child. It wasn't random curiosity, Alina. I have a genuine motivation for everything I ask.'

Her jaw firmed, her shoulders hitched. Bracing for what? The sight of her teeth giving a quick tug to the side of her mouth gave him a moment of regret, determinedly squashed. He needed facts.

'What did you imagine would happen when you requested a meeting?'

To his surprise she relaxed, as if she'd feared a different query.

'Springing a newborn niece or nephew on you didn't seem right, even though I don't think you can get DNA proof till then. I figured you'd appreciate time to get used to the idea—time to decide if your family wanted to adopt the—'

'*If* we wanted to adopt Louise's child?' In a second he was towering over her, six feet of instant fury directed solely at the woman recoiling from him.

A range of emotions flickered across her features. Resentment. Anger. Guilt?

She pushed herself upright, causing him to step back. 'Yes—*if.* You expect me to believe your parents will *welcome* this? Even *with* DNA proof?' She glared up at him, delightfully incensed, daring him to contradict her.

Stunned at her outburst, he felt his temper abate. His mother's perception of social standing… His father's snobbery… Their disapproval of his sister's marriage… All probably the reason Louise's miscarriages had been kept secret.

He spun round to the window, running agitated fingers into his hair. How much more angst was a man supposed to endure?

'Options were limited because of their attitude.'

Her tone was gentle, conciliatory. He turned.

'Louise knew they'd consider adopting a failure, although it *was* to be their last resort.'

'I'm not sure they'd have accepted a surrogate grandchild either,' he grated.

'They weren't going to find out.'

It had slipped out, and Alina couldn't retract the declaration.

A predatory gleam flared in his eyes. He moved quickly, trapping her against the settee, his breath fanning her face. She stood her ground, holding his gaze, hoping he couldn't sense her trepidation.

A long moment later he inclined his head. 'I suggest we sit, so you can explain exactly how the three of you intended to hide it from us.'

She didn't sit. She flopped, desperately trying to regroup. Extremely perceptive, he had a reputation for dealing strictly on the level. Though he might accept his parents' rigid viewpoint had been the incentive for all their secrecy and deception, he certainly hoped the trio hadn't broken any laws. That would definitely test his principles.

He also had a way of undermining her defences, honing in on sensitive secrets. Some were not for sharing.

She watched him settle, folding one leg onto the settee. His features indicated that he was cool, calm, and collected. His right fingers lightly drumming on his thigh proved otherwise.

Crunch time. Next week she'd probably be back in Spain, managing alone until October. She'd learned life's lessons the hard way, already had a plan worked out. There was the trust account Leon had set up, plus an Australian bank account she'd never accessed.

Wriggling into the corner, she tucked her feet up and challenged him. 'Then I can go to my hotel?'

'Yes. Tell me the basics. We'll discuss the rest later.' Milder tone. Persuasive.

He laid his arm along the back of the settee. A normal gesture, yet she had a sudden urge to slide into its embrace, lay her head on his shoulder, and let him take care of everything. Crazy notion. Not for her. *Ever.*

'They made a generous donation to a clinic that caters to low-income couples. The procedure was done under fictitious names, with Louise and me using the same one. We planned to travel around, avoid people we knew. As a patient, I'd use her name.'

She stopped, reluctant to continue as his posture changed. He'd jolted upright when she'd mentioned fictitious names, slowly shaking his head in disbelief. Now he sat still as stone, an incredulous stare in his dark blue eyes. Icy chills ran down her spine; cold sweat formed on her palms. He didn't approve—couldn't comprehend all they'd been through.

'We didn't hurt or cheat anyone. In fact the money we donated gave other couples a chance to realise their dream too.'

His lips compressed. 'What about doctors and scans? The birth? What if something had gone wrong? How many people did you intend to lie to?'

Alina's grip tightened till the ring she wore dug into her flesh. Damn fate and to heck with life. She'd finally found the courage to confront her dark solitude; to try and help someone else in despair. And now she'd been left with the fall-out on her own. *Again.* She curbed the tears threatening to fall. He'd probably dismiss them anyway.

'As few as possible. There was no reason to suppose this pregnancy and birth wouldn't be normal.' Apart from the fact that this tiny person growing inside her belonged to someone else. 'You can't possibly understand. You weren't there.'

He froze. She couldn't even detect any movement from his breathing. His black eyebrows were drawn together, his cobalt eyes dark and fathomless. He was justifiably shaken. Right now she didn't care. She wanted this night to end.

'No, I wasn't. They never gave me the chance to be.'

They were both silent for a moment, then he startled her by reaching out and taking her left hand in his. His thumb stroked over her gold ring.

'How old are you?'

'Thirty.'

'I'll turn thirty-six in December. You're not involved with anyone?'

She shook her head warily.

'No one else is aware of your surrogacy pact?'

A more emphatic shake.

His next words were spoken in a clear, resolute tone. 'Then as far as everyone's concerned, Alina, this child is ours.'

Her heart began to thump wildly. He was claiming the baby as his own. *Ours. Our baby.* She stared at their joined hands and remembered his earlier words. The best solution of all. More than she'd dared hope for. No need for adoption.

'And it's credible because you were in Spain at the right time.' A whisper…barely audible.

Ethan had still been struggling to make sense of it all even as he'd made his declaration. His sister and his best friend had been prepared to lie, even commit fraud, to become parents. He'd have done everything possible to help. They hadn't asked.

Instead, whatever their original intentions had been, he would now be the father of their child. His tenacious, practical persona, the one that had achieved corporate success, kicked in. He refocused on Alina. He'd give her no choice. She had to accept the optimum scenario he'd envisaged last night.

Her drawn face and drooping eyelids mirrored his own exhaustion. They'd both been bombarded with emotional stress since the accident. Maybe if he carried her into the bedroom they'd sleep peacefully, continue their conversation in the morning. Maybe if he cradled her in his arms they'd find comfort.

Bad idea. He swung his leg off the settee, stretched as he stood. Glanced at his watch.

'It's been gruelling for both of us.' *Like a manic rollercoaster.* 'And tomorrow won't be any easier. This suite has three bedrooms. You can sleep here or I'll escort you to your hotel.'

'I'd prefer my hotel.' She hesitated, bit her lip before resuming doggedly. 'We weren't being reckless. We'd have gone straight to the nearest medical facility at the slightest hint of any problem.'

Her eyes begged for understanding, and she held out her hands, palms up, in supplication. 'I'm not lying. We'd never have risked the baby's health. *Never.*'

'I don't doubt it.' He didn't. They'd concocted a crazy scheme, with holes you could drive a truck through, and yet he found himself believing that with luck on their side they might have succeeded.

He phoned for the hire car. She put her shoes on and went to the bathroom.

A little later Alina stood quietly in the doorway, watching him replace the mugs. For seven years she'd befriended few men, always kept things casual. From the moment they'd met, Ethan James had stirred feelings she tried not to acknowledge. She prayed it was a fleeting thing, caused by her condition. Gone after the birth. Entrusting her shattered heart to anyone would be too great a risk.

So how come that stupid organ was beating faster at the sight of his muscles tensing as he stretched up to the shelf? Why was she gawking at his broad shoulders? Why was she remembering the feel of his hand on her spine?

He turned, as if sensing her presence, smiled reassuringly. She smiled tentatively back. He walked to the door, picking up a laptop bag from the dining table and his jacket on the way.

'Driver's waiting. We'll discuss tomorrow in the car.'

They exited the elevator into an underground car park, where a flashy silver limousine waited. Ethan gave their destination to the chauffeur before joining her on the plush seat. She loved the texture of the soft leather, breathed in its potent aroma, enhanced by her escort's earthy cologne. The brush of his thigh on hers as he twisted to buckle himself in caused her to shift towards the door.

Talk. Any subject. Anything to distract her thoughts from the vitality of the man by her side.

'What happens after I've seen your doctor? Do I leave?' she asked, striving for a casual tone.

The glance he gave her was enigmatic. 'No.' Removing the computer from the bag at his feet, he placed it on his lap and activated it.

Was he crazy? Her staying would bring embarrassment to his family, cause conflict with his parents. Better she go, returning later in the year. No matter what agreement they made, this baby would be born in Australia.

'You stay with me. You signed a legal contract to carry and give birth to this child. The purpose of your scheme was to prevent that child from suffering any repercussions from its origin or circumstances. Nothing's changed.'

Corporate-speak. Direct. Uncompromising.

He turned the laptop, enabling her to see the document displayed. An insane impulse to laugh shook her. It was an application for a marriage licence, with the groom's details already entered on the left, her name and his address on the right.

She bit back a negative retort. Ethan James didn't play games. He dealt with every situation shrewdly, sweeping aside opposition with logic and unwavering perseverance. And that was what she was to him—a *situation*, to be processed with tact and practicality.

He set the laptop aside, turned towards her. She flinched as his hand splayed across her abdomen, sending a warm glow sliding from cell to cell. She couldn't tear her eyes from his touch.

His voice was honey-smooth, adamant.

'Alina, the baby you carry is my family. I can't—
I won't—permit this child to be born illegitimate.'

She sympathised, but he had no idea what he was demanding from her. The warmth faded, replaced by a cold chill. Another hand, so like his, had lain there, eagerly anticipating the movement of an unborn baby. Caring. Sharing. Taken from her with no warning.

Somewhere out in the real world a driver beeped his horn. She sensed Ethan studying her, could imagine his brain churning with arguments to reinforce his demand. For him her full compliance was essential. He'd accept nothing less.

His words might come from an innate sense of duty, but the passion in his voice proclaimed a deep brotherly love. She'd been a willing party to the covert plan to protect the baby's name. It was as essential now as it had been then. She consigned her memories to the deep pit where they belonged.

'This explains your interest in my papers. How long is it supposed to last?' It came out wrong. She hadn't meant to sound so cold, so detached. She certainly wasn't prepared for the pained look in his eyes.

'We've got seven months to sort out the future.

No one will be surprised if our sudden marriage doesn't survive long-term.' His hand left her stomach and cupped her chin. 'I won't force you to stay, and I swear you won't lose from this arrangement.'

He was right—because she'd already lost everything worthwhile. She'd bought a new gold ring because she hadn't been able to bear the sight or the feel of the original. Wearing it discouraged male attention. He offered a marriage of convenience. No intimacy. No permanency. An expedient arrangement, lasting long enough to convince everyone he was the father.

She couldn't tell him—couldn't tell anyone about the darkness. Remembering the past tore her apart. Speaking of it out loud was unthinkable. His way made sense. If they married, his paternity would be undisputed. He'd give this baby the love she was incapable of feeling.

'You give me your word that I can leave when *I* decide?'

Being nomadic, with no involvements, was the only way to prevent her life from being devastated again. Last year she'd occasionally been drawn into small-town activities. And she'd connected with Louise and offered her help, completely breaking her basic rules. Look where *that* had landed her.

'Yes.' It was blunt. His body was rigid, his features unreadable.

'All right. I'll marry you. When will it be?' So impersonal, so soulless. Why did that worry her?

'Tomorrow morning we'll collect the documents we need from your solicitor for a one o'clock meeting with the celebrant. She'll check the application, lodge it immediately, and the wedding will be a month later.'

He packed the computer into its bag.

As soon as legally permitted. Eleven years ago it had seemed to her like an eternity to wait.

CHAPTER FOUR

ETHAN CONTINUED TALKING as he unbuckled his seatbelt. 'I'll be here at eight-thirty in the morning.'

With a start she realised they'd reached her hotel. 'I'll be in the lobby.'

How did you say goodnight to the stranger you'd promised to marry? The day after you'd met? A man you'd never even kissed.

That last thought rattled her, and she tripped alighting from the vehicle. Ethan steadied her with an arm around her waist. She trembled from his touch—or her own agitation. She wasn't sure which.

'I'll see you to your room.'

He guided her through the foyer towards the elevators.

'It's quicker to walk up one flight,' she said, grateful no one else was there. His aroma mingled with hers, filling the space, heightening her already taut nerves.

He followed her into her room, his sharp, narrow-eyed appraisal of the decor rankling. To her dismay she sensed him making mental note of the mundane fixtures and colours. Her accommodation, definitely lower standard than his hotel, faced the rear of an office block. It was simply somewhere to shower and sleep for a few days.

'It's clean and comfortable,' she retorted. 'It suits my budget. So, if you've finished being critical, I'd like to get some sleep.'

'I'm not judging, Alina. By contacting me you have placed yourself and our child under *my* protection. That's the reason you can't stay here.'

He reached out to her. She stepped back, holding up her hand. She didn't have the inclination to pack even the few belongings she'd brought for a short stay. In addition, she needed some physical space between them to reinforce mental distance.

'Not tonight. I'll check out in the morning.'

His expression disheartened her.

'Please, Ethan,' she begged. 'Give me one night.'

He relented, let out a rough grunt. 'I've been pretty hard on you, haven't I? No more than on myself, I swear.'

He touched her cheek gently. 'I'll see you in the morning. May I have your mobile for a moment?'

He took it and programmed his number in.

'In case you need to contact me. Sometime to-morrow we'll transfer your phone to an Australian plan.' He brushed his lips on her forehead. 'Sleep well, Alina.'

She locked the door behind him. Leant her brow against it, her mind a fuddled whirlpool of every-thing they'd said and done, everything they hadn't, the way he'd looked, smelt and created minute fis-sures in her defences.

She filled out the breakfast menu, hooked it on the outside door handle, then sank wearily onto the bed, just for a few minutes. Tomorrow she'd need to be focused. Solicitor. Celebrant. Hazily she wondered what else he had planned.

He'd already booked the celebrant, arrogantly confident that she'd accept his proposal. Not that he'd actually *asked* her. She ought to…

Deep, dreamless sleep claimed her, held her de-spite the traffic noise. Held her through the alarm's whirl.

Ethan rested his head against the seat, staring un-seeing at the city buildings on the drive home. He'd wanted to kiss Alina Fletcher. Not the soft-touch goodnight kiss he'd given her prior to leaving, but full mouth-to-mouth contact. Another unexpected jolt to his system, and the reason he'd let her stay at her hotel.

His primal instinct to relocate her and shield her from any adverse action was logical. His nephew or niece—no, his *son or daughter*—deserved every resource at his command to ensure a safe and healthy start in life. The sexual attraction was another blindsider.

The women he dated would never settle for 'clean and comfortable' accommodation in any circumstances. The woman he'd coerced into marrying him was an enigma, hiding more than she revealed.

As he lay on his bed, reliving their conversation, the tight rein he kept on his emotions finally cracked. Images flickered through his brain like a movie screening: the secret signals between him and Louise at strict formal meals with his parents, late-night covert snacks watching clandestine television in his room. Her radiant face when she and Leon had confided they were in love. Boyhood games with his best mate, double-dating in their teens. Standing proudly beside him as best man at their wedding.

The dam broke. The tears flowed for his spontaneous, vibrant sister. For his brother-in-law, friend and confidant. For the beloved couple who would never hold and cherish their child.

He rolled over, buried his face into the pillow. Guttural, heart-wrenching sobs racked his body and soul.

Alina was already in the lobby when Ethan arrived fifteen minutes early the next morning. Her treacherous senses responded to his lithe movement as he strode across the pavement. She felt skittish, illogically animated, despite the stern talking-to she'd given herself as she'd showered and prepared to leave.

The delivery of her breakfast at seven-thirty had finally awoken her, still fully dressed on top of the bed. Years of routine had enabled her to shower, pack and be settling her account within an hour. Years of self-enforced solitude had her wishing she could hail a cab and run.

Stylishly dressed in tailored grey trousers and a short-sleeved dark green shirt, Ethan was halfway to the reception desk when he veered towards her. Her pulse skipped at the sight of his tanned muscular arms. Her cheeks flamed at the memory of his touch, his oh-so-light kiss on her brow. *Had* to be hormone madness. She refused to contemplate any alternative explanation.

'Good morning, Alina. You look refreshed. Sleep well?'

She recoiled from the full impact of the 'seduction smile' Louise had mentioned. Quickly recovered.

'Yes, thank you. I'm ready to go.' As she bent to collect her suitcase their fingers collided, adrenaline spiked. She jerked hers away at the same moment his body stiffened.

'Gentleman's prerogative,' he murmured, picking up both pieces of luggage.

She walked silently beside him to the street, where a chauffeur waited by the open boot of a limousine—same car, different driver.

'I'll programme the car hire number into your phone. Use it whenever you go out alone.' He glanced at her as he stowed her luggage. Quickly added, 'I appreciate you're used to being independent, but since Monday you and our child are my family. I take care of what's mine.'

For a moment she resented his over-protective attitude, before realising the baby took precedence. As it should. She'd agreed to live the Ethan James lifestyle so she'd have to adapt and conform.

'I'll try.'

'Thank you. We'll need your solicitor's address.' As they drove off towards the harbour tunnel he offered her his mobile. 'Call his office and arrange to have your papers ready for pick-up.'

'Already done. He'll see us when we arrive.' His surprised expression forced her to explain. More than she'd wanted to. 'I have his mobile number. He dealt with everything after… I was pathetically incapable of doing anything—couldn't make decisions, couldn't think. I…'

'Was reacting normally to grief.' His hand covered hers. 'I understand, Alina.'

'Um… He's a good man. His office is my Australian address.' *I shouldn't find your touch so comforting.*

'It might be expedient to change it to mine. You'll be living with me at least until next year.'

Living with him yet not together. Next year?

Too many decisions in too short a time.

'Can I decide later?' She met his gaze, found mild curiosity not censure.

'Of course. Speak up if you feel I'm rushing you.'

Like the leader of a stampede. Not an opinion he'd take kindly to.

She stared out of the window as the traffic

crawled along, reliving the incident in the lobby. Ethan had been looking down when their fingers touched. Had he noticed she'd removed her ring?

From the stories she'd heard, and the photos she'd seen, she'd formed a vague, admirable image of Louise's successful brother—had had no interest in knowing anything more. The man at her side was flesh and blood, solid and real. She was learning to gauge the inflections in his voice, to interpret the messages in his expressive blue eyes. Her body involuntarily responded to him. The image had been far safer for her mental stability.

Ethan held back when the solicitor greeted Alina with a hug and soft words, allowing them privacy. The handshake he received was firm, the assessing gaze slightly disconcerting. Was he being compared to her husband? This man knew the full story of her bereavement, had been there for her when... What about the Fletcher family? Where had *they* been? Where were they now?

He noticed movement at her side as they were led to a small office, arched his neck to confirm the nervous finger ritual. His heart lurched when her features crumpled at the sight of the archive box on the otherwise empty desk. Once they were alone she drew a long breath, before walking forward and lifting the lid with unsteady fingers.

On their return journey Ethan booted up his laptop. His gaze flicked from the screen to the box containing her life history, on the seat between them. Moved to her left hand. To her bare ring finger.

He was acutely aware of the toll the visit had taken on her. Her fumbling through the box's contents and forced shallow breathing had torn him apart. He still hadn't finished sorting the personal papers he'd brought from Spain.

Gently taking hold of her wrist, and letting what she held fall back inside, he had closed the lid. 'Not here. Not now.'

He'd lifted the box from the desk, then linked his fingers with hers. After speaking to her solicitor for a few minutes they'd left.

She hadn't spoken since she'd introduced him in the office, apart from a mumbled goodbye. Now, as their eyes met, she blinked, swiftly looked away. Primal instinct urged him to dump his laptop on the seat, wrap his arms around her and kiss her till the haunted expression in her eyes changed to—to what? Desire? Passion?

Get real, James. Where the hell is your head?

'I'm not being very helpful, am I? But I haven't needed to access them since probate was granted.'

He heard the slight accent in her trembling voice. Caused by deep emotion?

Putting his computer aside, he clasped her slender hands in his. 'Working hands. Not salon-pampered. Well-cared-for working hands,' he murmured. 'Seven years is a long time to be running and hurting. Finding yourself alone and pregnant so soon after you'd finally begun to connect again must have been traumatic, and yet you found the courage to confront me.'

She let out a tiny huff of a laugh. 'I considered you to be the approachable one in the family. I'd never have been brave enough to tackle your parents alone.'

'That will not happen,' he stated forcefully. 'I won't allow them to interfere, so we'll meet them together after the wedding. I have friends who'll be witnesses. Is there someone you'd like as yours? Family? Friend?'

She had an alluring, pensive air as she pondered his question. *Was* there anyone? There had to be relatives somewhere.

'I have no family. My mother left me with her parents when I was four. Never said who my father was. I haven't heard from her since. Grandma's cancer was quick and aggressive, the year after I finished school, and Grandpa had a heart attack three months later.'

Soulful violet eyes held his for a long, long moment; resolve flickered there, then glowed.

'There are a few people I've kept in touch with. I'll have to think.'

Her tension had eased and her voice was steadier. She appeared to have accepted the reality of their situation. His admiration for her grew, along with another indefinable impression.

'Our next appointment is at one,' he said hastily, not wanting to dwell on the effect she had on him. 'So we have plenty of time.' He released her, reached for his laptop. 'And I think you are brave enough for anything, Alina Fletcher.'

'Thank you.'

He was wrong, but Alina accepted his compliment rather than set him straight. He considered her courageous. Would he believe the same if he knew her decisions were driven by the conviction that she'd be unable to feel any maternal bonding ever again?

'I mean it. Coping with all this must be painful.'

He opened the box.

Excruciating. Like having old wounds ripped open with no anaesthetic. 'It had to happen sometime.' *And it must be now.*

She moved the box closer to her side. 'I'll find what we need.'

Her birth certificate and papers relevant to her mother were on the top, where they'd fallen. Nothing heartrending there. She passed them to him, willed her hands not to shake as she dragged a buff envelope from the bottom. She held her breath, forced herself to focus.

Concentrate on the two you need. Ignore the rest.

Icy fingers fisted round her heart. She clenched her teeth as she carefully removed two certificates. Tucking them under her hip, she waited until he'd finished entering information, then filed away the papers he'd used.

'I'll do the rest.' She heard the tremor in her tone, stubbornly persisted, needing to retain some privacy. Needing to keep the walls up and solid. 'It's *my* past.'

He studied her with an intensity that made her insides quiver. 'If you're sure?'

She wasn't. She had no choice. 'Thank you.'

He settled the computer on her lap, ensuring it

was stable. 'I understand.' He paused. 'You haven't eaten a lot this morning, have you? Fancy an early lunch?'

How could he tell? 'I had toast and fruit—enough after that lovely meal last night.' Truth was she'd had to force the food down, and she still wasn't hungry.

His eyebrows twitched almost imperceptibly. His interest wasn't for her alone. She let him win.

'Chicken salad with crusty bread sounds tempting. Will the dining room be open?'

'We'll have Room Service.' He pulled out his mobile.

She tuned him out as she typed names, locations, dates. She recited, *They are words, figures, nothing more* in her head. Her newly unadorned finger mocked the information she entered.

'Done,' he told her. 'We'll eat, then deal with the celebrant. Changing your phone supplier has to be done in person, so we'll combine that with a visit to the jeweller.'

She met the steely resolve in his eyes. He was locking her into her promise. There'd be no reneging allowed.

His mouth curved into a persuasive smile. 'It won't be so bad, Alina. You'll have time to adjust to life with me until the wedding. Any functions I ask you to attend during our marriage will be quiet occasions, with people I trust.'

'I made a list this morning.' That was better. Keep the conversation on standard stuff.

This time his eyebrows actually arched. 'What sort of list?'

'Things to do. Everyone who'll have to be notified that I'm relocating. Most of my official stuff goes to Crow's Nest.' She couldn't stop the catch coming into her voice. 'Louise used to check the mailbox in Barcelona for me sometimes.'

'We'll need to arrange for it to be redirected. Do you have a base there?'

'No, I rented rooms on a casual basis. When I was away the owner stored my stuff for a small fee.'

'We'll fly over later, so you can decide what to bring back.'

She gave a short, hollow laugh. He made it sound like a day trip to another state. 'Hardly worth a trip. There's just an old suitcase and two plastic boxes.'

His turn to be confounded. 'That's all you have?'

Shoot, she'd spoken impulsively to a very astute man. She pictured the cold steel unit she'd visited once, fought the hard clench in her abdomen. Couldn't lie. Couldn't look into those perceptive eyes either.

'Everything else I own is in storage. I don't go there.' Mentally *or* physically.

'Too painful.' He made it a statement.

Guilt tempered with empathy overrode her self-pity. His grief was new, raw, and he had to cope with the aftermath of the accident. He was processing the estate personally. She'd let her solicitor take charge.

'I'm sorry, Ethan. I haven't been very sympathetic to *your* loss. I've been too wrapped up in myself.' She covered his hand with hers. 'You've had so much to deal with and still managed to be patient with me.'

'That's easy.' His voice hummed with tenderness. He flipped his hand to enfold hers. 'You're carrying our child.' His sudden grin took her by surprise. 'Do you have a things-to-buy list?'

She responded with a light laugh. 'I've jotted down a few things. Why?'

'Just wondering. All done?'

She frowned, realised he was referring to the marriage application, and felt the lightness of the mood change.

'Not quite.' She returned to the keyboard and added the final data. When she looked up his head was averted, as it had been when he'd made the call.

'I've finished, Ethan. Thank you for giving me privacy.'

'No problem, Alina.'

The car pulled in to the kerb as he stowed the computer in its bag.

Their lunch was delivered to a family suite. Afterwards Alina watched TV while Ethan went to another room to take a phone call. She viewed without seeing or hearing. Was he *ever* off duty? Her guilt resurfaced. The time and effort he was devoting to her meant less for his expanding empire.

The telephone's ring made her jump. Should she answer it? Thankfully Ethan came through and told Reception to send their visitor up.

Too late to change her mind.

She swallowed the lump in her throat, tamped down her qualms. Steeled herself to act like a newly engaged woman. For his sister and brother-in-law. For their baby.

The celebrant was friendly, bright and efficient.

She guided them through the procedure, gracefully declined a drink and promised to lodge the paperwork immediately. The wedding was set for Sunday, April the twentieth at five p.m.

Within fifteen minutes of her departure they were on their way to his apartment.

CHAPTER FIVE

OPULENT WAS THE word that came to mind as Alina stood in her own lavish en suite. *This is my home until the end of the year.*

She ran her fingertips across the marble surfaces—pure, cool luxury—but felt wary of touching the shiny chrome taps in case she left marks.

Bright stunned eyes stared at her from the pristine mirror. Walls the palest of pale mint-green complemented darker green mottled floor tiles, the crystal-clear shower. Matching it all were the softest, fluffiest towels she'd ever snuggled her face into.

She washed her hands, massaged moisturiser into her skin, breathing in its mild perfume.

She loved the beautifully appointed bedroom too. Also with a green theme, nothing bright or glaring, and as tranquil as a country spring morning—including a painting of a clear stream flowing between banks of willow trees. It was her own calming space, where she might be able to achieve meditation.

Sitting cross-legged on the luxurious cream carpet, she rested her elbows on her knees. Shut her eyes. *Black terror.* They flew open. She concentrated on the rural scene. *Breathe in. Breathe out. Count slowly. Count the flowers in the grass. Count the trees or rocks. Block out everything else.* Her inner fears receded—a little.

She stretched, unravelling her legs to lie flat, gazing up at the downlights strategically recessed in the ceiling. By tucking her chin in tight she could see her toes. For how much longer? She rolled over to do twenty push-ups. Did the building have a gym? If she didn't work she'd need to start exercising more.

She brushed her hair and went to join Ethan in the spacious open living area. Too tidy. Too clean. To her, not lived-in. No magazines or books scattered around. No bowls of fruit or nuts. The only personal touches were two framed photos on one shelf of a too organised bookcase.

His dark hair showed over the top of the long red couch, his low, rich voice lured her forward. As if sensing her, he turned, spoke into the mobile held to his ear. 'Hang on a minute.' He covered the mouthpiece, studied her with reflective cobalt eyes. 'Okay?'

Her reward, when she nodded, was a full-blown lethal Ethan James smile that blew her composure sky-high. 'Give me ten minutes. If you're thirsty, I'll have coffee.'

The kitchen area was TV-cooking-show-perfection: black granite benchtops——including an island—with stainless steel appliances. It enforced her earlier assessment. His apartment contained top-of-the-range exclusives with a wood and leather theme. Had he given carte blanche to the same interior designer who'd decorated the hotel?

She hadn't cooked in a kitchen with an island since—since she'd sold the three-bedroom house, mortgaged to the hilt, that she still couldn't bear to see ever again. Not since hired contractors had packed up the contents and put them into storage arranged by her solicitor.

She clamped her teeth together and focused on the coffee machine—top-brand, naturally.

'Bronze pod for me. Biscuits in island cupboard. Top shelf.' His voice floated through the room, accompanied by soft clicks as he dialled another number.

Everything she needed, including a decorative

wooden box with the word 'TEA' inlaid on the lid, sat on the bench. She activated the machine for his coffee, then opened the box. A delighted 'Wow...' whispered from her lips. Her blind lucky dip into one of the sixteen compartments of herbal tea— some quite exotic—produced lemon and ginger.

Ethan waited while his project manager verified figures, his eyes tracking Alina as she made two trips, carrying mugs and a plate of biscuits into the lounge. There was nothing hurried in her movements—hadn't been from the moment they met. Except when he'd challenged her about her husband and her child.

His eyes did a slow full-body scan, from the short wavy hair framing her pretty face down to the sleek white blouse, over her still flat abdomen, over slender shapely hips, ending at dainty bare feet. His own body enjoyed every second of the journey.

Quiet and unassuming, she'd have been overshadowed by the vibrant Spanish women he'd chatted up on his visits. Or would she? She disturbed him in a sensual way, new and puzzling, and definitely unwanted in their current circumstances.

'Ethan? You still there?'

The voice in his ear jolted him out of his daydream. Reality ruled.

He gave due praise to his colleague for an urgent problem solved and ended the call. Dropping his mobile by the files on the table, he took an appreciative drink of the strong adrenaline-reviving coffee.

'Thanks for this.' The object of his distracting thoughts was now curled up in one of the lounge chairs with a notebook and pen, completely oblivious to the effect she had on him.

'What's the title of the latest?'

Alina frowned.

He indicated her notebook. 'List?'

'Ah… Personal items. Clothes. What I have won't do for living *your* lifestyle.'

Her voice held an audible hint of resignation that sparked a twinge of sympathy. He understood her reluctance, but couldn't change his stance. He was taking the only course of action he'd be able to live with, irrespective of personal preferences or consequences. Those must be considered collateral damage.

'I've ordered a credit card for you.' He held up his hand to stop her interjecting. 'No argument.

Having you here is my decision, so I'll cover any costs you incur because you're living with me.'

'I have money.'

Enticingly stubborn, eyes fiercely defiant, mouth so tantalisingly kissable…

He'd eventually win—just not easily. Every step was a walk in a minefield and they'd hardly entered the paddock. Knowing women as he did, he figured once she began to shop for her growing figure and new social commitments she'd realise he was right.

'Compromise? Accept the card. Use it at your own discretion.'

Her gaze shifted over his shoulder to the photos on the bookshelf. Leon and Louise on their wedding day. With him at a social event. Her eyes softened. She played it down but she'd cared for them too.

He watched neat white teeth bite into a chocolate-covered biscuit, inexplicably imagined them nibbling on his neck. Selecting a plain shortbread, he stretched his legs and crossed his ankles. Wondered what it was about her he found so fascinating.

'Compromise it is. I have final say,' she stated with determination, causing him to chuckle out loud. 'Is there a gym in the building? Or nearby. Until I find a job I'll—'

She stopped as if stunned when his body jerked forward. Coffee dregs splashed onto the table. His eyes narrowed.

A *job*? She wanted to *work*? Hell! He stood, drew in a ragged breath and quelled his exasperation.

'Wait.'

He strode to the kitchen, brought back a cloth and mopped up the mess. She watched him warily. How could he explain his world to a woman who'd depended only on herself for so long?

Sitting by her side, he took her hand in his, felt her resistance. Held on. 'In the social circles I grew up in few women worked. There was always a hint of condescension when my parents spoke of those who did—even those with a profession. My contemporaries are a mixture, mostly by choice. I make no judgement.'

He cupped and tilted her jaw until their eyes met.

'We are different. You've come to me two months pregnant, with limited work skills. Uh-uh.' He quickly placed his thumb over her lips as she stiffened. 'That was not an insult, merely a statement of fact. I admire the diverse ways you've supported yourself, but I'd like you to relax, indulge yourself while you are with me. Accept a little pampering. Let me take care of you both. Please.'

'I'm not sure I know how.'

Her wistful eyes confirmed her words. He waited, liking the way the violet darkened and her brow furrowed as she contemplated the idea.

'Does taking courses constitute work?'

Spontaneous laughter rose in his throat. She was adorable. He hugged her close, pressing his lips to her hair. Wanting to press them to hers.

Rising to his feet, he held out his hand. 'Come with me.'

She hesitated for a second, then accepted his offer. He led her through the kitchen into a short corridor, flicking a hand at two doors on the right.

'Storage and spare.' He opened the door on the left. 'But this is what clinched the deal for me.'

He watched her expression and wasn't disappointed. Her amazement duplicated his when he'd first walked into the not yet finished lap pool/gym area. One glance, one split second, and he'd contracted to buy.

She gawked at the neat array of exercise machines and banks of weights, at the long narrow strip of water. Her lips parted, but he quickly averted any speech with fingers over her mouth.

'Don't…'

Her eyebrows lifted as he spoke.

'Don't you dare say it.'

Her chin lifted defiantly. 'You have no idea what I was thinking,' she claimed into his skin.

He huffed. 'A comparison between our worlds and I refuse to listen to any more.'

She studied the equipment for a moment, then him, and damned if he could define the expression in her eyes. Though he sure as hell knew he wanted to change it.

'Our choices define us, Alina. This is one of my best. My sanctuary from long hours and constant electronic hassle.' He moved behind her, put his hands on her shoulders. 'Now it's yours too. I'll set up lighter weights on any of the machines you want to use. Do you have bathers with you?'

Bathers? Alina's eyebrows scrunched. She'd packed for one or two meetings with a workaholic businessman. The rest of her time would have been spent sightseeing. Depending on the sales, maybe she'd have bought a few bargains. At the last minute she'd thrown in her one evening dress.

She twisted her head to tell him she'd add them to her shopping list. Froze. Her movement had brought her lips close to his. Kissing close. Her legs became jelly. Her mouth as dry as autumn leaves. Her heartbeat a jungle drum message.

His earthy cologne, enhanced by the scent of musky male, encircled her. The hazel rims of his dilated pupils were clearly discernible. Hypnotic eyes drew her in. Heat from his body seared her back, even though their only contact was through his hands. Arousing warmth lured and yet frightened. Distantly familiar. New and alarming.

It was illogical to feel chilled and cheated when he abruptly let her go. Put distance between them.

'Use this area any time you like, though I'd prefer to be here while you do. If the water's too cold I'll up the temperature. Towels are in the cupboard by the door.'

General information, spoken matter-of-factly. He obviously wasn't bothered at all.

Illogical to feel disappointed that his main concern would be the baby's wellbeing. She vowed to make good use of the gym and pool whether he was there or not.

Ethan walked towards the door, berating himself for the rush of desire he'd felt when she'd turned to him. He had to find a way to block this impractical attraction. He chose his women carefully. No homebodies, no clingers. No romantics. Intelligent, beautiful; sometimes both. He shared pleasant evenings and satisfying nights with them. Nothing more.

Alina had no idea how she affected him. She'd probably fly back to Spain tomorrow if she knew what he'd been thinking. How he'd almost kissed her. How much he still wanted to.

Frustrating days, weeks, months loomed ahead. Enforced celibacy with Alina within reach. Limited touching. Yet making their story believable required getting personal, learning each other's personalities and habits. Fast. They had to present a united picture to everyone: a couple mutually attracted enough to have had an ardent fling. It wasn't happening at the moment.

He pivoted round, catching her elbows as she cannoned into him. 'You know something about me, courtesy of my sister. I'm still groping in the dark where you're concerned. So it's imperative you talk to me, lighten up when we're together.'

He slid one arm around her waist; saw apprehension cloud her eyes.

'We'll let people assume we were lovers...they'll believe I'm the father.' He skimmed his fingertips lightly across her cheek, murmured softly as he lowered his head. 'A man and a woman who've made a baby should at least act as if they've kissed.'

He covered her mouth with his, giving her no chance to thwart him. And his barely restrained libido ran riot. His arousal was swift, unstoppable. Tangling his fingers in her silken curls, he anchored her head while desperately fighting the urge to deepen the kiss.

Willing her lowered eyelids to open, he moved his lips over hers. Pressed a little harder. Her soft lips tasted sweet. Didn't respond.

Nice one, James. Great way to gain her cooperation and trust.

Did he imagine the light tremor under his hands? The tiniest motion of her lips? He eased away. Her eyelids fluttered, opened. His breakneck pulse cranked up another notch at the bemusement in her incredible violet eyes. Lord, he ached to have her even closer, moulded to his hardened form.

Worst idea ever.

He shifted, let his hand slide over her shoulder, down her arm. 'We'll work on it.'

She eyed him with suspicion as she pulled away. 'Yeah, like you need the practice.'

Her offhand comment might have succeeded, if not for its delightful breathless timbre. Deny it all she liked, she'd been affected by his kiss. He rubbed his nape, wishing he could dive into the clear cool water behind him. A few laps fully clothed might diminish his ardour and help regain his sanity. Instead he had another trip in an enclosed car with her by his side. With that too-strong, not-for-her perfume assailing his senses.

With supreme effort he brought the conversation back to household routine. 'The pool is cleaned regularly. The apartment is serviced Monday, Wednesday and Friday mornings. They process any dry cleaning I leave on the kitchen island.'

She looked dazed for a second, then welcomed his change of topic. 'You have security. How do I enter and leave?'

'I've ordered another key card. You can have my spare.' He checked his watch. 'Time to go. Can you be ready in ten minutes?'

Alina wasn't surprised when they were escorted to an exclusive room on the fourth floor above a renowned jewellery store. Entrance to the secure area was gained by virtue of a buzzer and inter-com system.

Ethan moved one of the four seats closer to hers, giving the impression of an attentive fiancé. She berated herself for tensing. How could they fool anyone into believing they were a couple?

An elegant, bespectacled man entered, offering congratulations as he placed two ring trays in front of them, another at the end of the cloth-covered table. Alina stared, stunned. Her body involuntarily tried to put distance between her and the brilliant array. The strong arm around her shoulders tightened as if Ethan sensed her agitation.

Dazzling gems in a myriad of colours and settings sparkled and gleamed. Too flashy for her... too many to choose from. There was no comparison to the small diamond in a heart setting that she'd chosen and been kissed over so long ago.

Don't think. Don't remember. This has nothing to do with reality and emotion.

Quiet words were spoken. The jeweller left with the two trays. He returned with a less ostentatious selection. She still couldn't choose, couldn't bring herself to touch.

Ethan caressed her cheek with his knuckles. 'Too much choice, sweetheart? May I?'

Noting his endearment, knowing it was for the benefit of their attendant, she managed a fleeting smile and leant back. She didn't dare speak in case the pain showed in her voice.

Without hesitation he selected an oval amethyst surrounded by tiny diamonds set in gold. Elegant, not showy. Her finger trembled as he guided it on, holding it firmly to stop it sliding off.

Raising her hand, he pressed his lips to her fingers. 'Perfect. Beautiful. *You.*' He kissed her gently.

She knew this was purely for show, knew she had a part to play. So she did what she'd struggled against by the pool. She returned his kiss.

Her heartbeat accelerated. Her body quivered. His hold tightened, his lips firmed. Her fingers crept up his neck, teasing the ends of his hair. She felt giddy, breathless. Cherished.

Until her stomach knotted and fear replaced the floating sensation. Heat flooded her cheeks; she broke away and bent her head to his chest.

Ethan framed her face with his hands, forced her to meet his gaze. Her warm blush was gratifying. Coupled with the soft glow in her violet eyes, it gave an idyllic image of a newly engaged woman.

His own feelings were elusive, and he had no inclination to analyse them here. They were new, overwhelming—might be caused by any one of the upheavals in his life.

He placed the ring to one side, before swapping

the tray for the one at the end of the table. 'Do you prefer a plain or patterned wedding band?'

He'd bet odds that the cross-cut patterned ring she chose was very different from the one she'd worn years ago—not the plain one she'd removed since yesterday. He selected a matching, broader one, then spoke to the jeweller.

'Mine fits. Alina's need to be resized.'

CHAPTER SIX

THEIR NEXT STOP, within walking distance, was his communications supplier. Somehow the end result was a new mobile for Alina with her account bundled with his. Ethan James had a charming way of overruling objections, leaving you feeling as if you'd done *him* a favour.

Like the way he'd cajoled her into an exclusive perfumery store after claiming that he'd noticed her spray bottle was nearly empty. When had *that* happened? Well aware that the one she wore, a Christmas gift, was too strong for her; she was delighted with the new delicate spring fragrance. She'd been aware of the surreptitious looks he'd exchanged with the assistant. What else was he planning?

The arrangements, phone calls, et cetera had all taken time and effort, yet he made it seem simple. To him it was. Decisions were made. Actions followed. Tangible proof of the attributes that had ensured his phenomenal success. Skill and diplomacy would ensure the optimum outcome: a healthy son or daughter.

On their way back to the apartment the car pulled in to the kerb and Ethan unclicked his seatbelt. 'Won't be long.'

He hopped out and the driver moved off. One lap of the block found him waiting to be picked up, now carrying two plastic bags containing rectangular objects with a delicious exotic aroma.

He laughed at her puzzled stare. 'Thai takeaway. Best in town.'

'But…' Of course—the call he'd made while the salesgirl had been demonstrating functions on her new phone.

'Nothing hot or spicy. And what we don't finish tonight we'll have tomorrow. I've had many a breakfast of reheated Asian food.'

So had she—more from the need to stretch a budget than for pleasure. She laughed as her stomach rumbled. 'I'm hungrier than I thought. Thank you for remembering about the spicy.'

'I remember everything you've told me, Alina.'

His eyes caught hers, held her spellbound. She fought to break the hold, had to stay detached. Letting him in was a risk with too high a cost.

* * *

She was happy when he opted to eat in the lounge, claiming casual dining made takeaway taste better. Watching television would provide a break from personal questions and conversation.

At his request she carried two glasses and a carafe of iced water into the lounge, while he brought china, cutlery and the food.

'Tonight it's your choice—apart from reality shows,' he remarked, scooping special fried rice onto two plates.

'I haven't watched much at all these last few years. Hey, not too much on mine.' She stilled his hand, preventing him from overloading the second plate. 'The news is fine by me.'

During the ad breaks they discussed the events of the day—small talk which gave her invaluable insight into the man she'd committed her immediate future to. He wasn't as complimentary about the present government as she'd expected, and spoke sympathetically about lower income earners.

The latter didn't surprise her; she'd experienced his attitude to shop assistants and his own hotel staff. He did surprise her when he patiently explained the intricacies of a technology breakthrough. So she chose a documentary next, figuring it would interest him, knowing she'd like it too. His avid interest in the excavation of an ancient English church which had revealed a former king's remains proved her right.

Ethan's attention strayed during the advertising breaks. Alina would have plenty of time to watch anything she liked in the coming months. It suddenly occurred to him that she'd need something to occupy the hours while he was working. Even if she did sign up for a course or two.

How many people in Sydney had she kept in touch with? Was there anyone she'd confided in? He couldn't imagine how he'd have got through his teens, resisting his parents' expectations, without Leon to confide in. Even Louise, five years younger and flighty as a cuckoo fledgling, had listened and supported him.

Alina had stayed away from Australia. Did that mean there were no close friends here? It was obvious that she carried a deep-seated torment inside. *Damn*, he knew so little about her, but he couldn't bring himself to push too much. He was supposed to be good with people. If he earned her trust maybe she'd confide in him. When he knew the details he was convinced he'd be able to find a way to ease her pain.

Alina stretched as the final credits rolled, then carried their plates to the dishwasher. Ethan followed with the glassware and caught her yawning.

'Ready for an early night? It's been a full-on day for you.' Sympathy showed in his eyes, warmth in his tender expression.

A restful soak in the bath with an intrigue novel appealed more than bed. Did that seem rude? As if she wanted to get away from him?

As if sensing her confusion, he gently took her in his arms, hugged her and let her go.

'Goodnight, Alina. Thank you for being so co-operative. I know it wasn't easy. Sleep well.'

'I survived. Goodnight.' She walked away.

'Alina?'

She turned at the doorway.

'I swear I'll take care of you and our child. Believe me?'

She looked into sincere blue eyes and her doubts subsided. 'Yes, I do.'

This time he didn't stop her, and went back to the lounge. Trying to read reports was a futile exercise. A few strides along the hall was a beautiful woman who stirred him as no one ever had. A woman whose soul-destroying sorrow influenced every decision she made.

Today she'd begun to react naturally—the way he needed her to if they were to convince everyone they'd been lovers. Their supposed affair might have been short, but their mutual attraction had to be evident. On his part it was becoming less of a pretence every time she was near. And from her tentative responses he suspected her buried feelings were beginning to emerge.

Ten past nine. Past morning rush hour. Alina leant on the island, checking her notepad, and glanced down at her well-worn jeans. Added two items to her list. She drank her ice-cold juice, scrunched her nose. Pushed the credit card Ethan had given her in a circle on the granite. Having it didn't mean using it.

He'd knocked on her door early this morning to tell her he was going to his office. Drowsy, needing to use the bathroom, she'd barely acknowledged his remarks. When he'd leaned in to brush her hair from her eyes, his unique smell and the touch of his fingertips had blown her lethargy away, leaving her wide-awake, tingling.

She dropped the pen. This was ridiculous. What could be simpler than writing a list of clothes and accessories to be worn by the wife of a hotshot billionaire? Or was he even richer? Any woman he dated would have no problem filling the page. But she was a nomad, with a meagre pile of cheap, easy-care clothing. Her serviceable underwear would never grace a magazine page or stir a man's libido.

Hey, what was she thinking?

Focus. You only have to buy enough to be presentable for a few weeks.

As she put on weight she'd have to shop again. More expense.

For a second her mind flashed to the investment account. Another buried secret.

Sometime after twelve she sank wearily into a window seat of a busy café. Two bags containing the pathetic results of her attempted retail therapy took the chair beside her. This was hopeless. She'd chickened out every time she'd tried to enter any of the high-fashion boutiques she'd found. Embarrassing Ethan in clothes from the stores she normally frequented wasn't an option. At this rate she'd be in track pants and baggy jumpers right through autumn.

She needed help…didn't know who to ask. She was used to working; now she had all day with nothing to do. Or did she? She'd meant her reference to taking courses as a joke, but now she deemed them a plausible time-filler.

As the waitress walked past, carrying two plates of fish and chips, another idea popped into her head. Taking out her notepad, she began a new list, pushing it aside when her order arrived.

Indulging in a gooey cream-filled pastry didn't solve her wardrobe problem but it tasted good. Drinking Viennese hot chocolate while writing the final items lifted her spirits. Surely he'd give her plenty of notice before expecting her to meet his friends or accompany him to functions?

Ethan sniffed appreciatively as he entered the apartment—later than he'd intended due to an impromptu meeting with his second-in-command. The sooner he implemented the new changes in his workload, the better.

It was a surprise to find the table set for two, even though he'd called, asking her to order dinner from the hotel. There was a bowl of fresh garden salad in the centre, and a bottle of Shiraz waiting to be opened. His home was warm and welcoming—a pleasurable new experience. He shed the trials of his day and moved forward.

'Mmm, smells good. Mushroom sauce, if I'm not mistaken.'

'Hi.' Alina came around the island, carrying water and glasses. 'Dinner will be ready by the time you wash up.'

Placing his laptop on the end of the table, he moved nearer, breathed in flowers and sunshine—perfect for her, enthralling for him. If this were real...

It wasn't.

This morning she'd been dreamy-eyed, and he'd come close to kissing her. He hadn't thought, had merely acted, something he'd need to curb if they were to build a trusting relationship.

'Give me five minutes.'

Alina arranged steak with foil-wrapped baked potatoes on warmed plates, placed hot crusty rolls in a serviette-lined basket. Smiled with satisfaction. Everything looked appetising, hopefully tasted as good. If she could convince him to let her cook and clean she'd feel so much better about their arrangement. Support for the child was one thing—her being totally dependent on him another.

No way was she going to compete with his qualified chefs. She'd serve recipes she felt capable of, even if they weren't gourmet standard. The cookbook she'd bought was for inspiration.

Ethan had already poured his glass of wine when she set down his plate, along with the gravy boat. When she returned with her meal he was waiting by her chair, studying his food across the table. She held her breath while he took his seat.

The sparkle in his eyes when they met hers was unnerving. 'This didn't come from my hotel kitchen, did it?'

'No.' She broke eye contact, her heart sinking. Took a sip of water. If the difference was so obvious she'd already lost.

'Hmm…' He poured gravy, put sour cream on his potato and began to eat.

Her breath caught behind the lump in her throat. Her whole body felt primed for his reaction. She so wanted his approval.

'It's good.' His smile caused her lungs to deflate, the lump to dissolve.

'Not what you're used to?'

'Better.'

She bristled. She didn't need or want pseudo-compliments. 'You don't have to butter me up. I know there's no comparison.'

'I promise I will always tell you the truth, Alina.

Since the accident I've ordered meals. They came. I ate often while still working, usually too focused on facts and figures to taste or enjoy it. At home I lived in a void. My way of blocking out the grief, I guess.'

That she understood. 'And I made it worse with my bombshell.'

'No—no way.' He dropped his knife, reached across and took her hand. 'It was as if nothing had real purpose. I avoided thinking about Louise and Leon because then I'd have to accept they were never coming back. I hated knowing I should have been there for them much more than I was.'

She laid her free hand on top of his, subconsciously acknowledging its male texture.

'You felt guilty? Oh, Ethan, there was never, ever, in any conversation I had with them, the slightest hint that you had been anything but a loving and supportive brother and friend. One who'd be there for them in a heartbeat if they needed you. I don't know why they kept their problem a secret. Maybe because shielding those you love from worry goes both ways.'

'Maybe. I keep wondering if there was anything else I could have done for them. All I know is that you've given my life meaning again. I wake in the morning knowing my sister and best friend aren't completely lost to me. I feel—'

He broke off, slowly withdrew his hand, as if unsure of revealing too much emotion.

'Best we eat while it's hot. What other culinary delights do you have planned?' He helped himself to a serving of salad.

'You mean it? You'll really need more than one meal to make a sound judgement.'

'Bring them on.'

His smile as he raised his drink ignited trails of heat along her veins, threatening the solid barriers she'd sworn to maintain.

'Here's to many more home-cooked dinners together.'

They clinked glasses. Alina let her water slide, cool and refreshing, down her throat.

'It's on the understanding that you tell me if it's not good or not to your taste. If I take over the housework as well it'll fill my days. I'm rethinking the courses idea.'

'I'm locked into a cleaning contract, so that's a different proposition. Anyway, in a few months you might be grateful for the help.'

And with the purchase he'd arranged today she might also reconsider.

She pondered his statement as she cut into her steak. 'You may be right. It's not easy work, but it pays the bills. Losing their hours here may cause hardship for someone.'

'You discuss what you'd like done with whoever comes. I'll notify the company that you have the authority.'

'Thank you.'

So she'd also done cleaning during her nomadic life, had not been too proud to accept domestic employment. Showed consideration for other manual workers. Every conversation gave Ethan more insight into her—thankfully without her realising how much she revealed.

'Are you a sports fan?' she asked. 'I know Leon and Louise were Sydney Swans supporters and watched the games on the internet. You don't appear to have much free time.'

'We never missed a home game when they were here. I'm still a fully paid-up member of the club, and get to go occasionally. It wasn't the same without them, and the Starburst Group has been growing, demanding more time. I often wind down at night watching whatever sport's being televised. Clears the mind.'

He asked which countries she'd been to as they

ate fruit and ice cream for dessert. She revealed that she'd become fluent in Spanish, Italian and French, got by in other languages, and considered it no big deal. His Spanish was basic, so to him it was an enviable achievement.

He made hot drinks while she stacked the dishwasher.

Alina struggled to keep awake during the short late newscast. Had to stop herself from falling against his shoulder and nodding off.

'Do you mind if I go to bed? I'm not usually so tired… It has to be the change of environment or the pregnancy, so hopefully it won't last long.'

'We'll check if you need extra vitamins on Monday. You go and rest.'

'Thank you.'

Admitting her failure at clothes shopping when he'd been so complimentary about her meal seemed a backward move. She'd try again tomorrow.

She had no idea that her disappointment showed in her face, but Ethan noticed, and couldn't resist drawing her into his arms for comfort.

'Dinner was delicious, Alina. I know this isn't easy for you, but I promise we'll work out any problems that arise. Tell me if anything bothers you and I'll try to put it right.'

Her eyes were bright as she accepted his vow, and without conscious effort he bent his head to kiss her, moving his lips softly over her mouth. He felt a slight movement in her lips, heard a muted sound from her throat. Reluctantly raising his head, he encountered bemusement tinged with sadness.

He relaxed his hold, stepped back and tried to keep his voice stable. 'Sleep well, Alina. I should be home earlier tomorrow.'

Watching her go, he cursed himself for his lack of restraint. Tonight they'd really begun to connect, and he feared she might rebuild her barriers overnight. He cursed his parents for the hang-ups that governed his thinking, tainted his ability to feel deep emotion with others apart from Louise and Leon.

His short, raw, ironic laugh was spontaneous. Those two had had no qualms about showing their love—privately or in public. Eye contact, touching, kissing—all had been as natural to them as breathing. He'd never, ever seen either of his parents show any tenderness for each other, never seen a sympathetic gesture like the one Alina had given him tonight.

Not wanting to dwell on why kissing Alina made him feel less alone, he reasoned doing it when they could be seen would substantiate their story of a short and overwhelming passion. But it had to be believable—from both of them. No holding back, no tension. He was a grown man, well able to curb any sexual urges.

Today had been better. Alina placed her special purchases on the coffee table before carrying the other bags into her bedroom. She'd still avoided high-fashion boutiques and exclusive salons, but with her more positive attitude she'd had some success.

In a big department store she'd found two summer dresses and a lightweight jacket to go with either of them on cooler days. The shoes and bag she'd bought also went with both. She had limited her new underwear purchases, knowing she'd soon outgrow them.

After showering and changing she settled in the lounge to be productive. She had a cup of tea, a block of nut chocolate and a home renovation show on the television. There was plenty of time before Ethan was due home.

His consideration might be because of the baby she carried, his attention and kisses might be to make their relationship more believable, but she had to admit she found them nice. Nothing more. She hadn't been cared for since she'd fled from Australia, too cowardly to face anyone or anything that raised painful memories.

Mentally planning tonight's dinner, she opened her present to herself...

CHAPTER SEVEN

SUBDUED NOISES CAME from the lounge as Ethan opened the front door—the earliest he'd been home for months. Putting his briefcase and packages down, he strode in. He hadn't let Alina know he was on his way, meaning to surprise her. Instead he was the one who stopped short, spellbound by the vision in front of him.

Alina was ensconced on the settee, her eyes lowered, completely absorbed in the material in her hands, her tucked-up legs hidden by a flowing pleated floral skirt. He took in the sleek line of her neck, the satin glow of her cheeks, the sweep of her dark brown lashes. A perfect picture of natural beauty, and for the rest of this year she was his to admire.

He stepped forward, willing her to look up, anxious not to startle her. Her own subtle aroma enhanced her new perfume, making his nostrils flare, stirring his blood. She sensed his presence, gave him a shy glad-to-see-you smile that zinged straight to his heart.

With two paces, completely forgetting his mental declaration of self-control, he was beside her, his arms around her. He bent his head, glimpsed the reticence in her eyes and somehow managed to pull back. Couldn't stop his grip intensifying, though.

'Ouch.' His left leg jerked. He massaged his thigh and chuckled. 'I've been slapped a few times. Never stabbed.'

Alina paled, staring at the small metal needle in her fingers. 'I… I'm sorry. I…you… I was sewing. You made me forget I…'

He took the offending weapon and placed it on the coffee table alongside an array of coloured thread. 'My fault. I was distracted by the entrancing sight on my settee. Didn't allow for hidden danger.'

She blushed at the compliment. 'It's not sharp. Do you want to check if there's bleeding?'

The nervous tremor in her voice, plus the remorse in her eyes, acted like a dousing of cold water. He'd shocked her, shamed himself. This macho being, acting on impulse, wasn't him. He couldn't explain even to himself, didn't know why.

He moved away, dragging his fingers through his hair, trying to concentrate on the essential reason for her presence in his apartment. Five days ago he'd had no idea she existed. To her he was the preferred solution to a situation she didn't want long-term.

Boardroom strategy—that was what he needed. He had to get back to his original plan. Convince everyone they'd been lovers. Keep his distance in private. Best solution for everyone—especially the woman observing him now with dark, cautious eyes.

He picked up the cloth stretched over a round wooden hoop from her lap. Various shades of green thread had already been woven into the outline of a country cottage garden.

'Interesting. Pretty scene.'

'Small, light, fits into my backpack and challenging enough to keep me occupied in the evenings.' She took it from him and laid it on the table. 'It's absorbing—stops me from thinking too much.'

'And you have a weapon handy if you're attacked,' he teased, standing up and pulling her to her feet. 'New dress? Beautiful.' His scroll from head to foot was deliberately quick, yet he still felt an appreciative clench. 'Good shopping trip?'

Her smile faded. 'Not my favourite occupation. Having no idea what size I'm going to be in a few weeks doesn't help. How was *your* day?'

'Busy. I received a delivery today. Let's sit down.'

She tensed as he reached into his inside pocket and brought out a small black box.

Taking her left hand in his, he slid the amethyst ring onto her finger. 'Perfect fit.'

She stared down at their joined hands. Her posture slumped.

'Alina.' Her head came up. He had a quick glimpse of sorrow, then it cleared. 'Remember why we're doing this. Who it's for.'

'I know.' She freed her hand then crossed her arms, hugging her body. 'It's… All this isn't what I expected.' Her mouth tried to form a smile. Didn't quite make it. 'I won't let you down.'

So brave, so determined to do the right thing, no matter how heart-wrenching her memories. So delightfully confused by her physical reaction to him.

Basic instinct urged him to hold her, protect her from more pain. But it wouldn't work for either of them. She wasn't going to stay. She had emotional baggage that his expectations of her were exacerbating. He had an agenda, an empire to build. He'd have a young child completely dependent on him.

He accepted he'd never be as approachable as his sister. She'd rebelled outwardly against their parents' attitude, defied them to marry the man she loved, and emigrated to escape their continued interference. He'd channelled everything into developing his company, determined never to emulate his parents and end up in a cold, loveless marriage.

Better to stay a bachelor, to enjoy female company without emotional entanglements. Strict rules and no pain when it ended. Becoming a single father at this stage might throw his life out of whack, testing him to the full, but he'd cope, adjust and succeed.

And on the topic of interference, Alina needed to be aware of a major factor.

'My parents won't be invited, so please don't wear the ring in public until after the wedding.'

She frowned, not understanding his meaning.

He explained. 'I've gathered Louise mentioned their attitude on social standing and—unbelievable in today's world—"breeding". They take snobbery to a new height. You're in or you're out, no middle ground.'

His gut clenched as he recalled their fights with Louise, their turning on him when he had defended her and Leon.

'They were never happy with Leon being my best friend because, although he was wealthy enough to give his children the best education affordable, his father had begun his working life as a bricklayer. His building firm is my main contractor, always will be. When Leon asked their permission to marry Louise they practically threw him out, forbade him from seeing her.'

'Which obviously didn't work. Couldn't they see how happy they were? How much he…he adored her?' Her voice faltered over the last few words.

'That didn't factor in their thinking. Our wedding may not be conventional, but I'd like it to be an occasion you'll remember fondly. There'll be no one there who might upset you in any way. Telling them afterwards gives them no choice but to accept that we're married.'

'I understand.' She began to slip the ring off. He stopped her.

'Keep it on at home. For me.' He brought her fingers to his lips for a second, then stood up. 'I've also got something to help occupy your time. Close your eyes.'

Alina had no fear of natural darkness. It was her own internal black world that tormented her. So, as soon as she sensed him leave she covered her eyes with her hands and opened them.

Shame at the way she'd swayed forward for his kiss, had almost succumbed to him, fizzed in her stomach. At the time she'd seemed to be weightless, floating, with no power over her limbs or her actions. She didn't resist. Didn't participate.

When he'd sprung away the bewilderment had had her blathering like a drunk, made worse by his shocked expression and deliberate retreat, putting distance between them. He'd recovered first, bringing normality back to the conversation, seemingly putting their embrace behind him.

That was what she had to do—act like a mature woman. She took long deep breaths, calming her stomach. Her defensive shields were solid. Mind you, if they began to crumble…

'Keep them shut.'

He'd returned.

'Or covered.'

Must be looking at her.

She heard some clunks, and the drag of the coffee table. The cushions dipped as he sat next to her. Now her stomach sizzled with suspense.

'This is for you.'

She stared in astonishment at the red laptop with

matching mouse and butterfly motif pad. Along-side lay a hardcover notebook plus a boxed set of pens. Her hand flew to her mouth.

Grinning broadly, Ethan gently lowered it, then lifted the computer's lid. 'The password's "bluesheen" at the moment.'

'You bought this for me?' Her incredulous gaze swung from his face to the laptop. Twice. She'd never had a computer of her own. Not with the nomadic life she lived. Though lately she'd been considering one of those lightweight notepads.

'All yours. Complete with bag so you can take it anywhere.'

She touched the keyboard cautiously, her fingers tripping across the keys. He caught one and pressed it on 'start'. The screen lit up and her eyes eagerly followed the process.

This was *hers*. Really hers. She turned to the man watching her with dark, hypnotic eyes. Swayed towards him again. Stopped. Touched his arm.

'Thank you.'

She was lost for words.

So was Ethan for a moment. His heart pumped and the lump in his throat threatened to choke him. He'd seen the intent to kiss him in those sparkling violet eyes, and perversely he rued her change of mind.

'You're welcome. Mouse or touch?' The connection for the wireless mouse was already in the port.

'I've always used a mouse. I'll have to learn to touch.'

Learn to touch him?

His chest tightened. He obviously hadn't listened to his own pep talk.

She quickly bent forward and began to type in the password; her hair only partially covering her reddening skin. He wasn't fooled by the action, and surmised she'd had the same thought.

'Why "bluesheen"?' The catch in her voice spoke volumes.

'Came out of the air.' *She'd been wearing blue the day they met.* 'Easily changed.'

'I love it. What are all these icons for?'

Her eyes shone with excitement, heightening his own pleasure.

'Finding out is part of the fun. I've added the internet, an email account and cloud backup.' He opened the notebook. 'All the passwords are written in here, plus relevant names with phone numbers—including my IT guy, who set it up. He's offered to give you one-on-one lessons if you like. I'm not too bad—he's brilliant.'

'Why? You know I won't be staying, so why are you doing this?'

He shrugged. 'Don't argue—just accept it. You can enrol for online courses…there's plenty to choose from.' He lightened the mood by joking. 'Imagine all the lists you'll be able to create. And you know you'll enjoy finding recipes.'

'You may not think so when you have to eat my weird concoctions.' She smiled back.

'I'll take my chances.'

His mobile rang. Bad timing. She was more at ease with him now than she'd ever been. Muttering a light curse, he wrenched the offending instrument out of his pocket, checked the caller. With a grimace he stood up.

'I have to take this. Do you have dinner planned?'

'Yes, but not started.'

'Save it for tomorrow. I'll book somewhere quiet where we can talk.' He got to the end of the lounge and glanced back, his dazzling smile sending heat-waves to every region of her body.

'You really do look exquisite, Alina.'

Another genuine compliment that gave her confidence another boost. It was hard to believe he'd bought her such a thoughtful gift she'd use in so many ways. The expense hardly registered with him. The time and effort he'd taken meant so much more.

Shutting down the laptop, she watched each process avidly, wanting to take in every little detail before carefully closing the lid. When she packed everything into the bag she found a charger and a set-up manual.

She'd intended to try shopping again tomorrow—now she'd rather stay home and browse. Anything she didn't understand would go on a list to be shown to Ethan. Although at least one session with his IT specialist was a must.

After putting her embroidery into a craft bag, she went to her room to give her minimal makeup a light touch-up.

As she walked along the hall the muffled mingling of running water with what sounded like a mistuned radio came through his door. Curiosity made her stop and press an ear to the wood. The slightly off-key singing persisted, too indistinct for her to recognise the vaguely familiar song.

The shower stopped. She scurried away, her cheeks burning. If he caught her would he be angry or amused?

She couldn't get that tune out of her head… couldn't remember the title. Couldn't ask him.

For Alina the family-owned restaurant with its discreet booth tables was ideal. She hadn't asked the name of the suburb; that would be making it a memory for keeping. Though, perversely, she knew she'd never forget the tasty meal, the restful music from the live band…her attentive escort.

Couples were moving on to the small dance floor and she watched them with envy. She had once known how it felt to be held tenderly, barely moving in a traditional lovers' slow shuffle. Without warning, images of all the women Ethan might have entertained here broke into her daydream. Stunning. Polished. Fashion connoisseurs who'd dance faultlessly.

'Hey.' His deep voice cut through her thoughts and she turned to meet his amused gaze. 'You're very pensive. Care to share?'

Not in a million years. The predictable warmth stole up her neck. 'Just enjoying the music. The meal was delicious. Is this a favourite haunt of yours?'

'A friend brought me here last year. I kept it in mind, waiting for a special occasion.' He put his hand invitingly, palm up, on the table. 'Never found one until today.'

Mesmerised by his incredible dark blue eyes, she laid her hand in his. He began to stroke her knuckles with his thumb. She dismissed the danger signals in her head. Her skin tingled from his touch. Her throat dried up, and liquid wasn't the solution.

Had she been so sensitive to male contact before? Had her hormones gone this crazy ten years ago? Those memories were locked away, never, ever to be revisited.

Ethan had seen her wistful expression as she watched the couples moving around the floor, her body swaying in time to the music. She was in another world. A long-lost world? He wanted her in the here and now, totally focused on *them*.

She'd provoked an acute rush of satisfaction when she'd given him her hand. His heartbeat had spiked, unaccustomed yearning snaking through him. The eons-old urge of man to protect his child? Or primitive gratification that its mother trusted him to safeguard them both?

'Dance with me, Alina.'

She glanced across the room, shook her head. 'I'll embarrass you. I only do modern stuff with no touching. Nothing like this.' She gestured towards the dancers. 'They are so graceful.'

'No touching *ever*?' His eyebrows rose in disbelief. 'Or only since…?' He left his question unfinished, didn't need a reply.

She tried to free her hand, merely succeeded in twisting it so that his thumb pressed into her palm. Stopped resisting when he resumed his slow caress. Was he playing fair? Touching and kissing hadn't been mentioned when they'd first made their agreement. There'd been no reason in that emotionless civil conversation.

'You're denying something you really want, Alina. Trust me. You'll regret it if you don't.'

Cautious eagerness dawned in her sceptical eyes. 'Your toes might regret it if I do.'

He laughed, walked round the table without letting her go. 'Let's find out.'

Drawing her to her feet, he led her onto the dance floor. He placed her left hand on his shoulder, his right hand on her waist, then clasped her free hand in his, over his heart. Each movement was slow, deliberate. Non-threatening to her peace of mind.

'Look at me, Alina.'

Alina did.

'Trust me.'

She did.

'Let me guide you.'

He held her firmly, murmured in her ear and directed her steps with his thighs. His breath tickled her earlobe, his cologne filled her nostrils. Heat radiated from his touch as he compensated for her initial stumbling. She let her muscles go loose, giving him full control of her movements.

They glided round the room as if floating on air. Her eyelids fluttered. The music combined with the man to create an ethereal realm she wished she could stay in for ever. No more sorrow. No more loneliness. She gave a soft sigh, glanced up—into a searing wave of cobalt desire.

Their feet stopped moving; their bodies swayed in time with the rhythm of the music. She couldn't swallow, couldn't breathe, yet she felt his deep intake of air. Felt…

Guilt—as strong and shattering as when she'd been the only survivor.

The magic dissolved into stark reality. She began to shudder—couldn't stop. She tried to pull away, found herself being ushered to their table and gently settled into her seat. The strong arm stayed around her, supportive, grounding.

A moment later there were muffled words in

a concerned tone, a deep reply. Deep as Ethan's voice but clipped, disconnected, not like him at all. She did know that it was his fingers lifting her chin, and hazily wondered why they trembled.

'Alina?'

She blinked, saw his pale face, his brow creased in concern. She bent her head, unable to find words to explain.

His hand dropped. 'Let's go home. We'll talk there.'

'No.' Plaintive, even to her own ears.

'We have to.' Soft-spoken. Decisive.

They drove home in silence. Alina counted cars as they passed, timed their stops at traffic lights—anything to keep from dwelling on the talk ahead. Could she feign a headache? Believable in the circumstances, but delaying the inevitable.

If Ethan James wanted to talk, they'd talk—sooner rather than later.

CHAPTER EIGHT

ETHAN KEPT HER hand in his after locking the car, only letting go to allow her to enter the apartment first. How come she'd not only become used to that small intimacy but welcomed it? She dropped her bag onto the island, walked round to make hot drinks.

'Would you like coffee?' She reached for a bronze pod.

'Make it a black pod. I need a strong kick.' He was already walking towards the hall, discarding his jacket as he went.

Good idea. She picked up her bag and headed for her room to change. Jeans and a casual top were more conducive to a serious discussion.

In the few minutes it took her he'd returned, and their drinks were ready in the lounge.

'Biscuits?'

She shook her head. 'No, thank you.'

His lips twitched at the corners, just a tad. 'Chocolate?'

So he'd noticed the wrappers in the bin and her stash in the cupboard. Again she declined. Why the heck was she being so formal? Last night the atmosphere had been light and friendly. Today even better. Until that moment when the past had reasserted its claim on her.

She sat in the corner of the settee, drawing her legs up tight when he chose one of the armchairs, putting extra space between them. She stared at the mug in her hands, dreading the words she might hear, fearing he might be annoyed if she couldn't or wouldn't answer.

'We have to talk, Alina.'

The sombre tone of his voice brought her head up. His eyes had the sharp intensity she remembered from when she'd taken over filling in the marriage application. As if reading her inner thoughts was the only thing that mattered at this moment.

'This isn't going to work the way we are now. I've never had a problem with women before, but now I'm second-guessing what to do. For our baby's sake we have to convince everyone we've had a passionate affair.'

'And I'm failing miserably. I'm sorry, Ethan. I don't know how… There was only ever… I…' The words wouldn't come. She bit the inside of her lip, looked down at her white knuckles gripping the hot mug.

His hollow laugh snapped her gaze back to his face.

'I'm not doing much better, Alina. I never knew grief could be so overwhelming, so soul-draining. You brought some light into my dark world. Now you're here—so sweet and beautiful, so vulnerable.'

He leant forward, hands clasped between spread knees.

'I can't deny the physical attraction. Can't fathom whether it's linked with knowing you're carrying Louise's baby. Tonight—the music, dancing with you in my arms—I was in a new world. I frightened you, and I'm sorry—'

'No. It wasn't you,' she cut in. 'There've been so many first-for-a-long-times for me, it's bewildering. I feel like I've been thrown back into mainstream city living without a guidebook.'

She suddenly realised she was mimicking his stance, sharing his desire for their plan to succeed. Something shifted inside her, as if the extra tightening around her heart that had come when she'd heard about Louise and Leon had slipped a few notches. The old pain remained. She'd accepted only death would bring *that* to an end.

'It's only been four days. I didn't expect to stay in Australia—much less with you.' She smiled, watched as his eyes softened and his brow cleared. His answering smile lifted her heart. 'I'm rusty in all the social niceties of sharing a home and… and things.'

He shifted as if to stand, sank back. 'I don't have a good track record there. I've only had two live-in relationships, neither here, and neither lasting more than five months. Both confirmed my belief that I'm not cut out for domesticity. I'm too prag-matic—and, as one of them pointed out, I've no romance in my soul. Assuming I *have* a soul.'

'That's better for us, isn't it?' Although did she really want him to stop his gentle touches, his scorching looks? His kisses?

'No.' Sharp. Instant.

He came to sit at the other end of the couch, fold-ing one leg up, spreading one arm along the back. She wriggled into her corner and listened.

'We need to create an illusion of instant attrac-tion and overpowering passion. I've never been de-monstrative with girlfriends in public. Little more than hand-holding and social greetings. So a good way to convince people our affair was different is to show affection in front of them.'

'You mean kiss if someone's watching?'

'Alina, we're implying that we had a short, tempestuous affair that resulted in your becoming pregnant. That you're here with me now will tell everyone you mean more than any other woman I've dated. Which is true in the nicest way. Our limited knowledge of each other doesn't matter—displaying our irresistible attraction does.'

'So somewhere between how we've been and how Louise and Leon were?' Not a hard task, considering the way she reacted to him each time they touched. As long as she kept her heart secure.

'Definitely less blatant—though I envied them their intimacy. I can't imagine having such a close bond with anyone. I'm aware I'll have to change the way I think and act, make it credible to friends and family. It's not only me who'll be affected by our success.'

She locked eyes with his. 'The baby.'

'*Our* baby. It's essential my parents believe that. You have to be comfortable with me as your partner, alone and in company.'

'I can.' She heard the slight tremor. 'I will be.' Better. Stronger.

Ethan slid his leg off the couch. 'Come here.'

That persuasive honey tone. Those compelling cobalt eyes.

She sidled along until there was barely a hand's length between them. His fingers lightly traced her cheek. His arm slid around her, loose yet secure.

'Any time you feel uneasy, tell me.'

His slow smile had her leaning in closer.

'Any time you feel like taking the initiative, go right ahead.'

He stroked her hair, laid her head on his shoulder and cradled her against his body. His heart beat strong and steady under her hand, an echo of hers. His voice, his cologne, everything about him was becoming familiar, safe. It was a feeling she refused to analyse.

'We'll keep to ourselves for a couple of weeks. When you're ready I'd like to arrange dinner with the couple I hope will agree to be our witnesses. If we're out and meet anyone I know I'll introduce you only by name. After the wedding I'll tell my parents, and then the whole world can know.'

'All at once?' she teased, liking the way his eyes crinkled at the corners when he laughed down at her.

She also liked the sound of the couple he went on

to describe—friends he'd known for years, who'd also known and visited Louise and Leon.

They made small talk, sat in quiet contemplation, still in an amicable embrace. When it was time to retire it was she who raised her face for his tender goodnight kiss.

Ethan leant against the wall, his gaze fixed on the light under her door, not quite sure what had happened tonight. A week ago he'd have claimed the scenario he'd suggested held no qualms for him, apart from the discomfort of their public displays.

He'd have bet his finest hotel that his romantic emotions would not have been involved, and still didn't quite believe they were. The trauma of losing his sister and best friend, the shock of Alina's pregnancy, plus his determination to take responsibility for the child were a formidable combination. It was enough to scramble anyone's senses.

He still believed his decisions had been made with logic and foresight, with the child's future wellbeing his main consideration. Main? He meant *only*. He'd be a single father, with all the problems that entailed. Public displays had to be kept objective—surface emotion only.

Yet he couldn't deny that Alina slipped under his guard whenever they were together, popped into his thoughts when they weren't.

The light went out. He whispered, 'Pleasant dreams...' and went to his big, lonely bed.

Alina woke early, had coffee brewing and the table set for breakfast by the time Ethan walked down the hallway dressed for work.

'Good morning.' He sat opposite and poured his favourite sugarbomb cereal. 'Do you want a lift anywhere this morning?'

'No.' Too quick. Too sharp.

Last night their decision had sounded plausible, simple to put into practice. This morning, as water had cascaded over her in the shower, she'd decided she wanted some alone time, to mull it over and fully accept its implications in her head.

'I'd like to practise on the laptop. I bet there are functions I've never heard of.'

'There are probably programs I've never used either. Any questions you have I'll try to answer later. With luck, and few interruptions, I might only need a few hours at the office.'

'Don't you usually work all day on Saturday?'

'Ah, that was the *old* me in the *old* days.' His

sparkling eyes belied his self-critical tone. 'A pre-baby workaholic. Now I'm in training to be the best daddy ever.' His voice roughened over the last sentence, and the sparkle dimmed a little.

Alina covered his hand with hers. 'You will be, Ethan. You'll be everything they'd want their child to have in a father.'

'And mother.'

She jerked her hand away. He caught it.

'There won't be any other. I sure as hell won't marry again just to provide maternal comfort or for the public two-parent image. I've learned from experience how a marriage held together purely for society standing can influence a child.'

That was why he'd have no problem letting her go, would never try to persuade her to stay.

There was no justification for the dejection that washed over her. No reason for the retort that burst from her.

'Louise turned out fine. She was generous, warm-hearted and open. Even through her medical traumas there was always a genuine welcome for anyone at their home. You know how everyone loved her because she was…was…*she was Louise.*'

'And I'm not like her?' He released her hand, picked up his spoon.

'I'm sorry. That's not what I meant.'

'No, but it's true. She never changed from the sweet, wide-eyed creature the nanny at the time put into my arms when I was five. She grabbed my finger, gurgled, and I immediately forgave her for not being the brother I wanted.'

His light laughter was tinged with remorse.

'I wish I'd been as courageous as her—constantly rebelling against the rigid conformity of our upbringing, openly making friends with people she liked, whether they were deemed acceptable or not. My way was quiet avoidance rather than personal confrontation.'

'You kept Leon's friendship, and championed them when they wanted to marry.'

He huffed. 'My parents didn't like that. I don't think they've forgiven me for supporting Louise's declaration that she'd happily have a park wedding without them. Not the "done thing" in their circle. It would have been embarrassing, so they capitulated.'

'Do you see them regularly?'

'We have little in common—different standards. They'd like me to be more involved in their close-knit elite group. I dislike the way they boast about my success to elevate their own status. They are, however, the only parents I have, so we maintain a polite relationship.'

He ate for a moment, eyes downcast. Pondering. Then looked up and spoke with determination.

'Forget them for now. Cutting down my office hours is essential to my being available for appointments right now, and planning for our baby in the future. So I've been reorganising my staff.'

'You're delegating?

'Even better—I've promoted. My second-in-command now has two assistant managers. Between the three of them they'll take most of the day-to-day load off me. By the time our baby comes everything should be working smoothly enough for me to take paternity leave.'

'Decision made. Action taken. Problem solved.'

'You don't approve?' He sounded disappointed.

'I do. Very much. It's so much a part of who you are. And it's been a long time since I've felt secure enough to depend on anyone for anything.'

She was paying him a compliment, saying what he should want to hear. Ethan shouldn't feel aggrieved, but he did. She admitted to trusting and relying on him—both important to their relationship. But he wanted something different, something more. Something indefinable.

He pushed back his chair, picked up his bowl.

'I'll clear. You head off,' Alina said, buttering a piece of cold toast.

'Okay. I should be home early afternoon. Did you buy bathers?'

'Yes, haven't worn them yet.'

He hadn't used the gym since Sunday. Or the pool since Tuesday evening, after their talk. He was normally a creature of habit and liked his routine, which included daily exercise and swimming early morning or evening. The less disruption, the less stress. If she worked out at the same time he'd know she was okay. It would be a start to getting his life back in control.

'How about when I get home? We'll work out, then swim.'

Her face lit up. 'That sounds good.'

He went to his room, planning a positive day. A few minutes later he collected his briefcase from his study, and left.

Alina ate her toast and honey, mulling over her every encounter with Ethan. She'd developed a habit of deep thinking over people and situations during her solitary lifestyle. Sometimes she created fictional stories about them in her mind to pass the time.

This was real. The attraction between them was real—had been since the moment she'd turned from that window. She could understand *her* reactions. Suddenly thrown into enforced proximity with an attractive, virile man after seven years alone... Pregnant, with rampant hormones playing havoc with her emotions...

His puzzled her. She appreciated the need for them to give the impression they'd been lovers, so kissing was essential. The first kiss had been experimental, to judge her response, the second for show. The others... She wasn't sure. Yet she'd sensed tension in him every time—right from the initial touch of his lips on hers. As if he was keeping a tight rein on his actions. Or on emotions he claimed not to have.

She sipped her camomile tea, pulled a face. Cold toast was okay—cold tea was not drinkable. It was time to get cracking.

She clicked on the kettle, cleared the table and set herself up for a morning's exploration of the internet.

* * *

The sound of the front door opening had Alina's head swinging round. A quick check of her watch surprised her. Ten to three. How could it be that late?

'Hi, you've set yourself up pretty well, there. Good use of the dining table.'

How did this man's smile make a good day seem brighter?

'Better than leaning over the coffee table. Did you get what you wanted done?'

'Finally—it took longer than I'd hoped.' He leant over her shoulder to check her screen. 'Agassi Falls? Planning a trip, Alina?'

'Just having fun surfing,' she replied. 'I checked out some courses, then spent some time finding out what all the icons stand for.'

'I trust you've been taking breaks and eating properly?' Banana peel lay in a small dish, alongside an empty mug on the table.

'Yes, sir. I've stretched every hour…done other stuff in between.' She arched her back and smiled up at him. 'This morning I went out for a short walk; this afternoon I went through your kitchen cupboards to see what's there before looking up some recipes. I found a few meals we might enjoy, but—'

'You can't print them out. We'll fix that on Monday, along with a desk and chair.' He held out a red USB. 'In the meantime copy and use mine.'

'Thank you.' She surprised both of them by rising up on her toes to kiss his cheek. 'This is all I need. You don't want to be left with excess stuff.'

Ethan opened his mouth to refute her claim. Changed his mind. Words weren't going to change hers.

'That's my concern. Right now I'm psyched up for the session in the gym we agreed on.' He took her hands, held her at arm's length. 'Hmm, nice tracksuit—you look as good in green as in blue. Give me five minutes.'

'I'll meet you there.'

He strode to his room, fantasising about the bathers she might be wearing under that outfit as he hastily pulled on T-shirt, bathers, track pants and sneakers. She was waiting for him, sitting on the press-ups bench. The lights were brighter than he usually set, the music a pleasant background sound.

'Bike or treadmill for warm-up?' she asked, offering him a bottle of water. 'I don't mind either.'

'I'll take the bike.' It was still set up for him. 'Twenty minutes okay?'

She agreed, and he selected a programme for mid-range difficulty. Settling into his normal pace was easy—resisting the temptation to watch Alina not so easy. She moved smoothly, gracefully.

'I promise I won't fall off.' She'd caught him checking her out.

'It's been a while since anyone's been here with me.'

Solitude in this special area had always been a plus. It was his private time, for releasing tension. Only occasionally had he invited anyone to join him. To his surprise, he didn't mind Alina being there at all. In fact he felt downright glad to have her running alongside him. A feeling that unnerved him a little, causing him to switch back to getting-to-know-you mode.

'What sort of keep-fit do you do on the move?'

'Depends on the current job. Crop-picking, dog-walking or waitressing are usually enough. If it's in an office I run, or do casual sessions at pools or gyms.'

'Whoa—back up. Dog-walking?'

Her laugh, the first genuine one she'd given,

zipped through him. Musical and light, it was a sound he wanted to hear again. Often.

'It's fun, challenging or downright exhausting, depending on the size or number of pooches. And always available in any city, any country.'

'Ever lose any?' The more he learned, the more fascinated he became.

CHAPTER NINE

'NO. I HAD one Labrador who didn't want to go back to his owner, but I didn't blame him. The woman's perfume was so overpowering it clogged my throat.'

She blushed and bent her head. So delightfully embarrassed he wanted to jump off and comfort her.

'Hey, yours just didn't suit *you*. On another woman it'd be different.'

'Someone more flamboyant? More "out there"? It was a Christmas gift from a temporary boss, probably recycled. The box had been opened.'

'Now you have the perfect fragrance for you— delicate, reminding me of sunshine and flowers. Ethereal...' He chuckled. 'Maybe not the last one. Though sometimes you *do* drift off into another world.'

Alina was grateful for the distinct ping announcing the end of her programme. She stepped off as the machine slowed down. Moved over to the weights.

For the next thirty minutes they rarely spoke, each concentrating on their own exercises. She'd have been completely relaxed if she'd been able to block out the male effortlessly lifting weights alongside her, built well enough to play A-league football.

He smiled whenever their eyes met in the huge wall mirror, disconcerting her. His T-shirt moulded to his sculpted chest and muscular upper arms. Her breath hitched every time his biceps firmed as he curled or lifted weights. She felt hot, sweaty, much more than she ever had while exercising before.

Deciding she'd done enough, she walked over to the pool. Discarding her tracksuit, she used the ladder, shivering as she descended into the cool water. Made a mental note to ask him to up the temperature. Taking a deep breath, she ducked under, sinking to the bottom, then shooting up. She grabbed the rail, shaking her head, refilling her lungs… Found herself staring at a pair of slender feet attached to tanned legs with a light covering of black hair.

She tilted her head for a slow scan past firm

calves to the muscular thighs that had steered her round the dance floor last night…and a pair of black swimming trunks that left no doubt as to his manhood.

Her mouth dried; her pulse raced. Her body heat overrode the chill from the surrounding water. She didn't dare meet his eyes, chose the coward's path and swung into a freestyle stroke away from him. Quickened her pace at the sound of a splash behind her.

Ethan overtook her, touched and turned at the end. He was still below the surface as they passed again. She recovered her composure, slowed to her normal leisurely pace. This wasn't a contest.

Six laps were enough for her.

She sat on the top of the ladder, wrapped in a towel, her feet dangling. She ought to leave. Shower and dress. Think about dinner—no, too early for that. She stayed. Not sure why, except that it was mesmerising, watching Ethan churn through the water, hardly making a ripple. The way he went through life: single-minded, controlled.

He swam like a machine—clean, even strokes, powering along the pool, flipping like a seal at the end. She timed his push-offs. Always constant. So precise. So coordinated.

She frowned. He'd dipped in front of her on his last turn, hadn't resurfaced. Suddenly he burst upward from the water, making her jump. His chest skimmed her legs as he rose, catching hold of the rail for stability.

'Waiting for me?' He grinned, spraying her with tiny drops as he shook his head.

'Hey!'

He levered himself higher so they were on eye level. 'It's only water. Anything special you'd like to do tomorrow? We'll have all day.'

'Oh. No work or commitments?'

'None. I'm all yours. Stay home, and relax. Go for a drive. Walk on the beach. Your choice.'

How was she supposed to make an instant decision with him so close that there was a hint of his cologne in the chlorine-scented air? With his glistening muscled torso inches from her twitching fingers? With his appealing blue eyes offering her something she refused to name?

'A ferry ride.' Out of the blue. From somewhere in her past.

His eyebrows almost met his dripping hairline. 'You want to go on a ferry?'

She nodded. 'The Manly Ferry across the heads. I used to love it during the winter in rough weather.'

His smile shot into a scowl. 'No *way* are you going out in a storm.' Grated out. Possessive.

She laughed, recognising the over-protective tone. 'They don't cross in really rough weather. I don't get seasick. And it's spring.'

He relented, didn't look convinced. 'We'll decide at Circular Quay.'

He twisted, hoisted himself out onto the pool side and picked up the towel he'd left nearby. Alina stood, heading for the door as he patted excess water from his body. He caught her arm and took her towel from her.

'Stand still.'

He moved behind her, began to dry her hair, firmly yet gently. It was soporific, soothing. She arched her neck in pleasure, sighed when he dropped the towel and began to massage her neck and shoulders. Trembled when his hot breath teased the pulse under her ear.

'Your muscles are taut as a drum. A proper massage might help.'

From *him*? Considering he was the main reason for their tension, she doubted it, but his offer was tempting.

'There's a beauty parlour in the next block. Make an appointment.'

Why had it suddenly become less appealing?

After Alina had retired for the night Ethan turned off the television and dimmed the lights. Then, sipping brandy, his feet up on the coffee table, he tried to make sense of the mayhem his normally ordered life had become.

He was committed to becoming a short-term husband and a lifelong father. He was becoming attached to a woman whose heart and love belonged to a dead guy. Her response to him was merely physical. His carefully planned future was now a day-by-day unknown.

Ethan suggested they put light coats, plus anything else she wanted to take, into her backpack—which *he'd* carry. He deliberately lingered over breakfast, determined to use their outing to ease any tension between them, make this a day for light conversation with no conflict.

It was mid-morning as they strolled towards Circular Quay. After guiding her across the first road he linked their fingers, claiming it would prevent them from being separated by the crowds already building up. She didn't argue, seemed content to let him be protective. He was rapidly becoming more comfortable with the feeling.

Had to curb it when, while drinking water and watching the boats, she declared she'd love to do the Harbour Bridge climb.

Alina hadn't *forgotten* the sheer joy of crossing the heads to Manly on a windy day in choppy seas. She'd purposely blocked it from her mind. Now she realised how much she'd missed the city she'd lived in for so many years.

Today it was fairly mild, until they reached the gap leading to the ocean. She felt alive, leaning on the rail, facing into the breeze, letting it prickle her skin and tease her hair. Nautical toots and engine noise, calls from yachts as they sailed past, all combined with the sounds of circling seagulls to fill her world.

'There's nothing like this anywhere—nothing so exhilarating.' She twisted her head to smile up at Ethan, braced behind her, his hands on the rail either side of her.

His expression said he didn't quite agree. She turned back, leant well forward, as if searching, unsure how to express the way she felt. He repeatedly said that he owed her, but she hadn't expected him to show it so personally, to spend so much time with her. Covering her living costs would have been ample.

'Hey.' One arm wrapped round her. 'It's a long way down.'

'I'm looking for dolphins.'

'Wrong area for them. Wrong season for whales.'

Husky tone, hot breath fanning her ear.

'Some friends and I did a whale-watching trip along the coast a few years ago. Mid-June, I think. If you're feeling up to it, we'll go.'

'I'd love it.' She let him draw her back against his chest. Breathed in the salty air. And him. Let herself live in the moment.

Ethan wondered if she knew how captivating she looked. Genuinely happy, with flushed cheeks and sparkling eyes, she was irresistible. He made a mental note to arrange a day's sailing with friends.

He cupped her cheek, bringing her face round to his. 'Nothing like it. Definitely no sight more beautiful,' he murmured, dipping his head to capture her mouth. He saw her eyes darken. Felt her tremble. Silently agreed: it *was* exhilarating.

The ferry lurched, breaking them apart. He grabbed the rail again, trapping her safely between his arms. They rocked in unison as the boat ploughed through the rough swell. General conversation might be safer.

'I have to confess the only ferries I've been on for years have been for corporate evening events with catered food and drinks. My friends and I used to think day-old pies and cold cans of drink were the ultimate meal.'

He realised how many other simple pleasures he'd left behind as he built his Starburst chain. Pleasures Alina understood and still enjoyed. His adrenaline surged at the thought of her helping him rediscover them. Then she'd go, leaving him to share them with their child. He trembled at the challenge.

Alina felt it and looked round.

'That wind's cold. Do you want to go inside?' he said.

He wasn't lying. It went right through the jacket he'd put on before boarding. Hers wasn't much heavier.

'You're kidding? Inside is for sensitive people, small children or the wuss breed. There's hot drinks and delicious fish and chips waiting near the docks.'

She turned back to watch their approach into Manly.

Ethan nestled his head against hers. 'Okay, but if I catch a chill you have to nurse me.'

The sound she gave was suspiciously like a giggle. 'No chance. No virus would dare attack you without an appointment.'

He stiffened. Was that the impression he gave? Good humour won him over. A week ago she'd been wary of him, anxious about his reaction to her pregnancy. Ready with a plan to have the baby alone if he denied her. He felt a warm glow deep in his gut. If she liked him enough to bait him he must be doing something right.

So he had a reputation for being hardnosed in business? He also was known for being fair and trustworthy.

Late on Monday morning Alina walked through the foyer, trying to pep-talk away her apprehension. Exercising hadn't helped. The line between truth and tacit lies seemed so tenuous. She was not the biological mother—had to persuade everyone she was. She and Ethan had never been lovers, had shared only a few kisses—one long one for an observer's benefit. Were required to act as if they'd had a passionate affair.

Her trepidation had increased when she'd realised he'd been rescheduling appointments to accommodate her and the problems she'd brought him. This morning he'd left early for a meeting postponed from Wednesday. Thirty minutes ago he'd phoned to ask her to come down and meet the car as he'd be running late.

For the baby. For Louise and Leon.

Repeating her mantra silently, she went outside to wait in the shade, praying he wasn't stuck in a traffic jam. The vehicle pulled in to the kerb as if summoned by her plea. She hurried forward, not giving the driver a chance to alight. Scrambling in, she dragged the door shut, leaving Ethan leaning forward awkwardly with his arm extended.

'Oh, sorry.' She gulped in a quick breath, inhaled his distinctive cologne. Flicked him an apologetic grin. 'I'm not used to having someone take care of me.'

'That lesson I'm learning.' Cobalt eyes appraised her as the car moved off. 'You look anxious, Alina.' He caressed her jaw line, tilted her chin.

'What do you expe—?'

He cut off her rebuke by firmly pressing his lips to hers. Her heartbeat hiccupped, doubled in speed. Sent her blood racing along her veins.

The kiss lasted less than a moment. Or for ever.

Too long. Too short. She slumped against the seat and stared at him, too befuddled to think coherently. The piercing eyes holding hers hostage showed no sign of the turmoil he'd inflicted.

She consciously steadied her breathing. 'You should warn me.' It came out like a husky plea for more rather than a reproach.

Ethan gave a low chuckle that resonated over her skin and skittered down her spine. 'So it's okay to kiss you any time as long as I don't surprise you?'

His amusement stretched already taut nerves. 'That's not what I meant.' She scrunched her eyes and bit on her lip.

'I'm not insensitive, Alina.' He lifted his hand. Let it drop. 'Every time I touch you I'm very aware of how you feel. Remember we need to portray a couple who can't resist each other?'

For him it was all for public image, so his declaration should please, not disappoint. Stupid hormones. She *so* had to check with the doctor why they were affecting her this way. In private.

'I can handle the pretence.' *Liar.* 'I'm getting used to it.' *Double liar.* 'It's… The doctor might ask for information I can't…can't give.'

'Ah…'

As if he understood. She shook with frustration.

'No, you don't get it. I can give her the dates she'll need, fudge the method of conception. It's… She's bound to ask…'

It had been bad enough writing details on the clinic's patient information forms he'd accessed on Friday. She'd thanked him for his considerate action in allowing her to fill out her medical history privately. It was the idea of it being voiced out loud that was eating at her. There was no way to explain the dark place where she'd buried the unbearable pain and heartbreak.

He wrapped his arms around her, drew her into his warmth. His hands began a soothing caress over her spine.

His voice was gentle, as if speaking to a child. 'You're not alone, Alina. I'll be with you.' His hands stilled. 'Unless you *want* to see her alone.'

Of course she did.

'No, that's cowardly. I can handle it.' Her quivering voice proved otherwise.

'Are you sure?'

He meant it. And the compassion in his blue eyes and the generosity of his offer gave her strength.

'You may have questions too. Besides, the father has the right to be there.' With a jolt of amazement, she realised a simple truth. 'I'd *like* you to be there.'

'I am the father...' His large hand covered her abdomen. 'My baby. Our child.'

She didn't protest and he appeared satisfied. She'd never be able to use that phrase, never be able to care that way again. Hearing it resonate from him relieved her. He was going be a great father.

Ethan linked his fingers with hers as they entered the light, hospitable clinic. Her anxiety was palpable and he had no remedy. Give him a struggling business to rescue any time.

'Relax, Alina. It's only a preliminary examination.'

At least his words earned him a faint smile. He steered her into an empty elevator and pressed the button. The compulsion to comfort her and drive the shadows from her soulful eyes rippled through him.

'We're bending the truth for our child's sake, Alina. The book claims doctors need dates and medical history—nothing more. No one's going to pry into your personal history.'

Her eyes widened in astonishment. 'What book?'

'The one I bought Tuesday morning, specifically written for expectant fathers.' His mouth twisted. 'Very informative and downright scary.'

They stopped and he guided her out.

She handed in the forms and her obligatory urine sample at Reception and were directed to an empty waiting room. Light classical music played softly in the background. Alina sat idly flipping the pages of a magazine. Ethan filled two plastic cups from an orange juice dispenser and offered one to her.

She accepted it with a noticeably shaky hand and his heart sank. He noticed her agitated finger movements, half hidden by the bag on her lap, finishing in a clenched fist. Hoping their appointment wasn't delayed, he put his cup on the low table and wrapped steadying fingers around her hand.

'Patricia Conlan has a very good reputation.' He raised the hand clasping the cup to her lips. 'Now, drink. Slowly.'

Alina obeyed, emptying the cup. He drained his, took both cups to a bin, then returned to sit beside her, studying a poster on the wall opposite.

She kept her eyes downcast, wishing she had his self-discipline. He'd been predictably shaken by her initial bombshell, and angry a few times during subsequent conversations, but he'd rapidly recovered his composure every time. She, on the other hand, had trouble keeping any control over her emotions.

She glanced sideways, surprised to find him looking more nervous than he'd let on. The long supple fingers of his right hand thrummed on his thigh, and she recalled them spanning her stomach. The image of them sensuously exploring her body flashed into her brain, and she couldn't stifle a throaty gasp.

He jerked round. 'Alina, are you all right?'

'Alina Fletcher?'

She jumped up, willing her burning cheeks to cool, grateful for the interruption from the uniformed woman in the doorway.

They were ushered into the consulting room.

'Dr Conlan will be with you in… Ah, here she is.'

'Alina, Ethan. It's nice to meet you.' The fortyish woman with slightly mussed brown hair and bright blue eyes clasped her hands, then Ethan's, in genuine welcome.

'Let's sit down and get acquainted.' She emanated compassion and invited trust.

'Thank you, Dr Conlan.' Alina took a seat, placing her handbag on the floor as a folder was opened and perused. Even Ethan's reassurance couldn't dispel her feeling of foreboding at the thought of queries about her past. An occasional note was written, an occasional 'hmm' mouthed.

She noticed a slight resemblance to her husband's Aunt Jean, triggering a pang of guilt. She'd only kept in token touch with everyone, had avoided personal contact. In a few weeks she'd have to notify them that she was living in Sydney. Remarried. Having another baby. The latter when Ethan decided to make the announcement.

Sneaking a peek at him, she met genuine concern. Whatever he saw caused him to take her hand, link their fingers and squeeze. He had no idea how calming those slight actions were.

Dr Conlan laid down her pen and glasses, placed her elbows on her desk and linked her fingers. She smiled sympathetically.

'I appreciate this must revive painful memories for you, Alina, and I sincerely hope your new baby brings you happiness.'

Ethan squeezed her hand again.

'The sample you brought in officially confirms your pregnancy. If you'd like to go into the examination area, I'll be in shortly. We'll talk after.'

Alina went to the open doorway indicated. The

faint murmur of voices drifted in as she prepared and lay down on the examining table. She stared at the ceiling, silently chanting her mantra.

CHAPTER TEN

NICE AS THE doctor was, Alina felt relieved as they left. A referral for an ultrasound and an appointment card were in her handbag. Ethan held the door open, his free hand clasping the pamphlets they'd been given.

She'd seen his surreptitious peek at his watch in the elevator. Catching his arm she stopped them both. 'You need to get back to the office, don't you?'

'There's always work to be done. We can—'

'Hail a taxi and I'll drop you off. The sooner you get back, the less chance of staying late.' And she'd have some quiet contemplation time to mull over the doctor's advice, read those pamphlets, and fully accept the path she'd chosen.

His cobalt eyes gleamed with gratitude. His fingers rested gently on her cheek for a moment. 'Spoken like a true corporate wife.' He looked round. 'There's a snack bar over there. I'll grab a sandwich to eat at my desk.'

He made one call during the taxi ride to his office, booking the ultrasound for Monday the twenty-first of April at ten. She wrote the date and time in her notebook as he repeated them for confirmation, realising it was the day after the wedding. When she would be recorded as his wife.

Ethan sensed a change in her. Was she too beginning to realise the enormity of their agreement, so simple in words, so complex and mind-boggling in reality? In front of the doctor he'd claimed to be the father of her child. He'd said 'our baby', 'our child' so easily. Now he had to fulfil the promises he'd made to Alina and his sister's memory.

His pragmatic nature demanded everything be put in place quickly, privately. Nothing left to chance, no hesitation that might give anyone cause to believe he doubted his paternity. Even before she'd agreed he'd set up appointments without considering the effect on her. Even after learning of her loss he hadn't deviated from his plan.

He hadn't allowed for the reality—hadn't understood the impact it would have on them both.

He reached for her hand, breathed in her sweet fragrance. She didn't react; lost in a world he had no right to access.

The taxi was nearing his office. He tilted her

chin, took in her subdued expression and almost told the driver to keep going. What could he say or do? Nothing until she was ready to confide in him. A quick kiss on her forehead produced little response. He had no right or reason to be disappointed. Only a week ago he'd walked out on her.

Alina's head was inside the kitchen island cupboard when the intercom buzzed at about eleven the next morning. She'd just managed to reach the small can in the back corner and jerked at the sound, banging her head.

She walked over to the front door. Hesitated. Ethan hadn't mentioned anyone coming. Would he want her to answer? Another buzz. She pressed.

'Hello.'

'Good morning. Is Ethan at home?'

The hairs on the back of her neck lifted at the high-pitched, cultured voice. Her mouth dried. She swallowed twice, rubbed her neck. Finally managed a croaky reply. 'No, I'm sorry, he's not.'

'I'm Sophia James. May I come up?'

His mother—judgemental to the nth degree. Far worse than the ex-girlfriend she'd suspected. Should she let her in? What would she do if Alina refused her entry?

'Hello? Are you still there?' Slightly peeved.

'Please come up.' Denial only delayed the inevitable. In three weeks Sophia would be her mother-in-law. For a short time anyway.

She raced to her bedroom to check her appearance. After brushing her already neat hair she went slowly back, taking long lung-filling breaths. Waited, slowly counted to nine after the bell rang before opening the door.

Sophia James was the epitome of a stylish, sixtyish woman with all the resources to fight any sign of ageing. From her coiffured dark hair to the handmade high-heeled shoes colours matched, everything fitted perfectly. There was nothing soft about her at all. Not a trace of warmth in her red lips or in her flat brown eyes.

Alina felt an irrational zing of satisfaction that both this woman's children had expressive blue eyes, clearly inherited from another family member.

'Please come in,' she said, standing aside.

Sophia walked in with an air of entitlement, scanning the area as if it were her territory. Scanning Alina as if she were an applicant for a lowly household position.

'You are not the cleaner. Why isn't Ethan here with you?'

Spoken as if she couldn't be trusted to be alone in his home. She felt a twinge of insecurity, then pride came to her rescue. She lifted her chin, squared her shoulders. *She's Ethan's mother. Treat her with respect. She's the baby's grandmother.* That last thought eased her resentment. This lady would *not* take kindly to any of the traditional titles given to a grandmother.

'I'm Alina Fletcher. Would you like coffee or tea? Ethan's at work.' She held back on saying, *But I'll bet you know that.*

'Mild coffee, thank you. White. No sugar.' As if she were ordering from a waitress in a café.

Alina watched as Sophia stopped before entering the lounge, giving the area a thorough scrutiny before selecting one of the armchairs. Giving the impression that she had never seen the decor before. After popping a pod into the machine Alina joined her, staying on her feet to attend to the drinks.

'You're the girl with Ethan in the photograph a friend texted to me. You were kissing in the street, and now you're acting like this is your home. Are you *living* with him?' Blunt and insulting.

She made a point of staring at Alina's bare left

hand, made no attempt to hide her displeasure. Alina's attitude swung again. How dared this woman question and insult her?

'I don't discuss my private business with strangers.'

Sophia's lips thinned, almost disappeared. Her back stiffened. 'I'm his mother. I have a right to know.'

'Then perhaps you should ask *him*. Next time we're in contact I'll ask him to get in touch.'

It was a definite dismissal. Forget coffee. Alina wanted her gone.

The scathing look Sophia gave her was defused by the dull shade of red flooding her face. She rose stiffly to her feet.

'Be warned, Ms Fletcher. You don't fit. You may have him fooled for a short time, but his contemporaries will see through you as easily as I do.'

Her movement to the door was as near to a stomp as Alina had ever seen anyone do in heels. She followed, far enough behind so that Sophia had to open the door herself.

She turned for a parting shot. 'Even suitable girls don't seem to last long with Ethan. Your novelty will quickly pall for a man of my son's impeccable taste.'

She swept out, leaving the door open.

Alina closed it, shaking with disbelief. She uncurled her clasped fingers to enable them to rub the back of her neck, tilted her head to the ceiling. What had she done? Apart from insulting his mother, and practically throwing her out of his home, she'd given the impression she had authority here.

Ethan hadn't wanted his parents to know about her yet. A public kiss hardly equated domestic cohabitation. Should she have lied?

Her head reeled.

Should she wait 'til he came home to tell him, when she'd be able to see his reaction? What if Sophia rang him first with a distorted version of events?

Taking bites of some dark rich chocolate for courage, she debated the pros and cons...

'She *what*?' The outrage in Ethan's voice seared down the phone line. She'd got no further than telling him his mother had visited before he'd exploded.

'I'm sorry, Ethan. I didn't know whether to let her in. I—'

'She's never been there before—never been invited. What did she want?' Barked out, agitating her even more.

'Someone sent her a photo of us kissing. I didn't know what to tell her.'

She'd screwed up. No, he'd put her in that position by keeping her a secret. It was *his* family who had the issues.

'You should contact her. I... I... I'll see you tonight.'

She hung up.

'Alina?'

She'd gone. Ethan realised his knuckles were white from his grip on the mobile phone. His free fist ground onto his desk. She'd sounded distressed. What the hell had his mother said to her?

He'd never been so angry. Or so worried when Alina didn't answer his call back. He selected his mother's number.

'Ethan, we haven't heard from you for a while.'

Not since they'd criticised the wording for the gravestone. Lucky for her there was half a city between them else he'd be tempted to throttle her.

'So you thought you'd pop into my home when you knew I wasn't there?'

She spluttered. He gave her no chance to refute his claim.

'Don't bother denying it. My receptionist logged the same female voice yesterday, saying she might call in. Your voice is quite distinctive.'

It wasn't said as a compliment. Anyone who truly knew him would have been wary of his low, controlled tone.

'I was worried. I'd received a photograph of you with that girl I met in your apartment.'

He almost lost it at her throwaway reference to Alina. Gritted his teeth, needing to know how his mother had discovered she was there. He waited for a long, tense moment.

'Okay, I described her to an acquaintance who lives a few floors below you. She said she'd seen her—sometimes alone, sometimes with you. I'm only looking out for your welfare, Ethan. There's something not quite right about her. She just about ordered me out.'

'After, I'm guessing, you began to interrogate her. Listen carefully, Mother. You'll have no more contact with me at all if you bother Alina again. Understand?'

'Ethan, you—'

'Goodbye, Mother.'

He dragged his fingers through his hair. *Alina, sweetheart, you didn't deserve that. I made a mistake—should have known she'd start digging at the slightest rumour I might be dating.*

He tried the apartment. No answer. Tried Alina's number twice more. It went to voicemail each time.

There was no sound in the apartment, no sign of Alina. Her mobile lay on the kitchen island. *She has to be here. Has to be.*

Ethan strode to her bedroom. The breath he felt he'd been holding for ever whooshed out at the sight of her handbag by her dressing table. Her bathroom door was open. Not there. One place left to check.

The gym area was silent apart from the low hum of the water pumps. The lights were dimmed, giving him limited vision of the figure floating in the pool. The only movements were slight flicks of her feet, gently propelling her along towards him. A rush of relief swamped his body. He sagged against the doorjamb, his heart racing. He'd had no reason to think she would run, yet he'd feared she might.

Wiping his hand over his mouth, he wondered why this fragile, damaged woman stirred him as no one ever had. It went deeper than the embryo she carried. His anger towards his mother had been at her treatment of Alina. His concern had been solely for Alina's feelings.

He toed off his shoes, stripped to his boxer shorts, watching her slow progress through the water. Not wanting to startle her, he walked along the side, meeting her halfway. Felt his lips curl. How did she keep a straight line with closed eyes?

They flew open, though he'd swear he'd never made a sound. Her head turned. One look into sorrowful violet and he dived in, surfacing next to her. He hauled her into his arms, the anxiety he'd experienced giving his action more force than he'd intended.

He buried his head in her neck, his lips seeking her pulse, his heart rate lifting at the feel of its erratic beat. The feel of her hands clasping his shoulders, her legs brushing his as they trod water, the tantalising aroma from her skin—all heightened his senses.

Her wrists stiffened, preventing him from drawing her closer. He raised his head, meeting censure in her eyes.

'Alina, I...' Where the hell were the words he needed? 'You hung up on me. Didn't answer your phone.'

Indignation flared, making the colour of her eyes even more stunning. Her hands lifted and slammed onto his skin, clearing his mind. He huffed out air, drew in fresh breath, regained control.

'I'm not angry, Alina—not at you. You sounded so upset. When you didn't pick up I was…' *Admit it .Tell her how you felt.* 'I'm not sure what I felt. Just knew I had to see you, hold you.'

'Your mother—'

'Had no right to come here. If I'd even suspected she might I'd have told you not to grant her entry. I'm sorry, Alina—and, believe me, so is she right now.'

'You've talked to her?'

His chest tightened. Hadn't she believed him when he'd said he'd protect her?

'More like a short, angry lecture. Plus her one and only warning. I made it clear if she upsets you again I'll have even less contact with them.'

'That's a bit drastic. They're your family, Ethan. I knew about her attitude, so I shouldn't have over-reacted—though she certainly lived up to her reputation.' Her tone softened with regret. 'I'm really messing up your life, aren't I?'

He shook his head. 'Quite the opposite, Alina

Fletcher. You enrich my life every day. You and our baby have changed my world.'

Her hands relaxed, allowing him to tighten his hold, bringing them into full body contact. Her fingers traced a featherlight path up his neck, across his chin. A glimmer of desire flickered in her eyes. It was satisfying for a few seconds—until his body responded to the flimsy barrier of cotton bathers and silk boxers between them, to the press of her breasts on his bare chest. To the flesh-on-flesh contact of their thighs.

His mouth crashed down on hers. No preamble, no gentle brush of lips—this was need, satisfying a hunger that had been building for days. From that first gut-clench, that first look into her haunted eyes.

He tilted her head for better contact, took what she offered, his tongue caressing hers, tangling, tasting the sweetness he'd dreamt of. And she was an active participant, giving and receiving, her fingers weaving into his hair, holding his head to hers.

His heart thumping, pulses pounding at every point, his lungs screaming for air, he had never felt so gloriously alive.

Reluctantly breaking the kiss, still holding her close, he gazed into violet eyes as bright as the stars in a moonless night, stunned and bewildered by the ardency of their kiss. He'd crossed an un-spoken boundary, knew he should apologise. Knew it would be a lie.

'Do you want another apology?'

How could Alina ask an apology of him when she'd willingly contributed to the kiss? When she'd seen the concern in his eyes as he'd surfaced be-side her? When it had been him she'd been think-ing of as she'd floated in the semi-darkness, lost in a hopeless fantasy?

There'd been no sound—only a crackling in the air surrounding her skin. She'd opened her eyes and dream had become reality. A splash and a mo-ment later she'd been enveloped in strong arms, his lips nuzzling her neck.

As if nothing had happened. As if his mother hadn't treated her with contempt. She'd bristled, hit him in an effort to get away.

His sincere contrition had chastened her; his de-fence of her had quelled her resentment. His claim that she enhanced his life had spun her back into her daydream and his kiss had been everything she'd imagined and more. She could no longer deny that she wanted him—rampantly hormonal or for real. Where that took them, she had no idea.

'I don't ever want you to say sorry unless you truly mean it. I'm the one who ought to apologise, for acting like an immature schoolgirl. I should have kept calm this morning and placated her.'

She was blurting out waffle, keeping back the words she really wanted to say.

The incongruity of the situation suddenly hit her. She was in a dimly lit pool, treading water with an almost naked, definitely aroused man whose very presence threatened her safe, isolated, un-emotional existence.

'Ethan, I… I can't… Oh, hell, I can't shop.'

Ethan's eyes widened when she swore. His hold loosened, giving her the chance to paddle back-wards, putting distance between them. He caught her at the steps, his touch light yet compelling. His hand framed her cheek. His little finger lifted her chin, enabling him to study her face with the intensity she no longer found intimidating. Espe-cially when the warm, caring gleam in his dark blue eyes said he'd wait as long as it took for her to confide in him.

She quivered: from his look, from his hold, from her fear of his reaction. From everything about him.

His lips curled in reassurance. 'If I let you go

now, will you explain what that meant when you're dry and dressed?'

When she'd had time to rethink, time to decide to try again. When he'd be corporately attired, in his business persona again.

Her eyes blurred with tears. She needed help— the sooner the better.

'Of course I can shop—that's ridiculous. It's buying stuff to wear when I meet the people in your world that's so daunting. Those fancy boutiques scare me; even the upmarket department stores are discouraging if you don't follow the latest trends. Reading magazines doesn't help, because I have no idea what's suitable for what event.'

'I like you in blue.' Instant and believable. He gently wiped the corners of her eyes with his thumb. 'And your new dresses look great.'

'They were easy. Summer daywear. Once I start meeting people you know I'll be judged on how I look, what I wear. How I speak. I'm afraid I'll fail you.'

Her mouth stayed open, unable to form more words as her brain seized on her last thought. Failing Ethan, having her unsuitable image impact on him, was her number one fear. Perhaps an avoidable situation if one woman had behaved as a loving mother should.

'Why couldn't your mother be more like Louise? Then I'd be able to ask *her* for help.' As soon as the words were spoken she wished them back. Gave a choked snort of a laugh.

'Stupid question. If she were we wouldn't be having this conversation. I need to manage by myself.'

CHAPTER ELEVEN

ETHAN HAD LOST track of the number of times he'd been racked with guilt these last several weeks. There'd been days when it had been as prevalent as breathing.

He'd given Alina a credit card, assuming she'd enjoy shopping. A lot of the women he knew—including his mother—considered having unlimited credit their due right, an essential element in their pursuit of looking stunning on the arm of their partner at any public or private function.

Alina was different. No demands, no preconceived notions. Absolutely no idea how beautiful she was.

He placed his hands on her waist, lifted her onto the side of the pool, and checked his watch.

'We'll meet in the lounge in, say, thirty minutes?'

'For what?'

His pulse hiked at the endearing way her brow

wrinkled and her eyes narrowed, as if she expected a reprimand.

'A shopping trip. If I'm the one you're dressing for, I guess I ought to help in the selection.'

His reward was a beaming smile and sparkling eyes—worth any amount of waiting outside changing rooms or carrying umpteen promotional bags. The single experience he'd had accompanying a female shopper had left him disinclined for a repeat, but this was for Alina.

'You mean it?'

He ran his finger down her cheek. 'I told you—I take care of what's mine.'

She was on her feet in an instant, grabbing a towel on the way to the door. He followed, hoisting himself from the water, giving himself a quick dry-off before retrieving his clothes.

It wasn't working. Ethan felt way out of his depth, wished he'd offered to find someone else to help her. He knew when a woman looked chic, understood the way it transformed her inner attitude. The selected clothes weren't having that effect on Alina. They were in the third boutique, and she'd modelled the tenth outfit.

The assistants had been helpful, yet there was an

edge to their attitude he couldn't fathom. Was it him? His obvious antipathy to this environment? Was it sweet, shy Alina, who hadn't looked comfortable at all, posing awkwardly as if she'd rather be anywhere else?

If she lifted her chin, held her shoulders back and stood proud, the effect would be so much better. He groaned inside. He'd promised to help her—failure wasn't an option.

'This isn't working, is it?

Her voice echoed his thoughts as she came up behind him, wearing the dress she'd left home in. He swung round, ready to protest.

Alina stopped his words with two fingers on his lips, ignoring the tingles her action generated.

'You're uncomfortable with it all, and I'm as helpful as seagulls at a beach picnic. I can tell what clothes *aren't* right on me. Others...' She shrugged. 'I have pictures in my head of women attending special events, can't put myself there. Maybe if you lend me some of your confidence it'll solve the problem.'

He gave her a crooked grin and took her hand. 'Not such a good suggestion, huh? I overestimated my expertise with all this. Louise was never a fashion slave, she—'

His eyes lit up, and his smile turned into a heart-stopping grin.

'I'm an *idiot*. Though, in my defence, I've had a few distractions.' He brushed his lips over hers. 'You being number one. Wait here.'

He was back in a few moments, after talking to the head saleswoman. As they left he pulled his mobile from his inside pocket.

'Got your notepad and pen?'

By the time she'd found them, his call had been answered.

'Thanks, Tanya…we're getting there. How are you? Definitely—we'll make it soon. Right now, I need the names of a couple of boutiques Louise patronised. It's for someone special who's recently moved to Sydney.'

He repeated three names and numbers for Alina to write down, promised to arrange a foursome dinner soon, then said goodbye.

'Don't know why I didn't think of her earlier.' He gently flicked her chin. 'Like I said—distractions. She recommends the first one, says the woman there has an uncanny knack of finding the perfect outfit for her customers. Let's ring—find out if she can see us today.'

* * *

Maralena's displays were simple, yet very effective, with one model in an appropriate setting in each window. Alina's fingers gripped Ethan's as they entered. She had no doubt how she'd be perceived, how the sales staff would wonder what he saw in her, why he was with her. She received an encouraging squeeze. What she needed was a little of his innate self-assurance.

Inside, there was room to move easily around the minimal racks of clothing, or along the walls containing full-length gowns. The blonde woman who came to meet them was everything Alina wished she was: poised and perfectly groomed, yet clearly approachable. She dispelled any fears with her genuine smile.

'Welcome to Maralena's.' She held out her hand to Ethan. 'Mr James, please accept my deepest sympathy for your loss. Louise always brightened our day when she came shopping, whether she purchased or not.'

'Thank you, she's very much missed. Please, call me Ethan.' He drew Alina forward. 'This is Alina Fletcher, her friend from Spain.'

'I'm Marlena—I tweaked the name a little for business. I'm pleased to meet you, Alina.'

She shook hands, then stood back, giving her
new customer a quick and thorough appraisal. Unlike Sophia's critical gaze, it was a professional
assessment which didn't bother her at all. To her
surprise, the eyes that met hers were approving.

'It will be a pleasure to help you, Alina. Do you
have any particular style in mind? Any colour preferences?'

All doubt dissipated, as if Alina's whole body
gave a sigh of relief. She'd found the help she so
desperately needed.

'I have a list of what I *think* I need.' She sensed
Ethan's lips curling. Was tempted to nudge him
in the ribs with her elbow. 'I've been backpack-
ing through Europe for a long time, so I'm out of
touch with what's in fashion.'

'What suits you is more important. Do you have
a time limit today?'

'No.' Emphatic from Ethan. 'Take all the time
you want.'

A few minutes ago Alina might have begged
him to stay. Now she had no qualms about placing herself in Marlena's hands.

She put her hand on his arm, drew him aside.
'Thank you, Ethan, this is just what I've been hop-

ing to find. You can go back to your office now. I'll be fine.'

His eyes narrowed. He didn't seem convinced.

'Did you leave work unfinished and come home because you thought I was upset?'

'No, because I *knew* you were.'

'I'm not now. The quicker you get back, the earlier you'll come home.'

He grinned. 'Can't fight feminine logic. Okay, I'll go. Call the hire car when you've finished.'

'I promise.'

He kissed her, slow and tender, seemingly oblivious to anyone else in the shop. Her fingers tightened on the strap of her bag, her other hand lifted to cradle his neck. Her lips moved in unison with his.

She felt his muscles tense. Wasn't this a kiss for show? To her it seemed the perfect place. Maybe he didn't, so she broke away.

'I'll see you later.'

'Mmm...' He blinked and his head jerked. Still holding her, he nodded to Marlena. 'Take care of her.' With a final squeeze of her hand, and a husky, 'Tonight...' he walked away.

'Okay, Alina, let's see your list.'

She was escorted into a dressing room. Within

minutes she'd confided her lack of success and doubts of her fashion abilities to an empathetic Marlena.

Ethan's mobile rang as he walked into the apartment building a few minutes before seven. Things were settling into place, with the agenda set for a breakfast meeting with his new management team in the morning. Once they were clear on their roles he'd be able to reorganise his working hours.

'Good evening, Father.'

'Ethan. I believe you have a new girlfriend?'

'Yes.' He wondered what spin his mother had put on today's events.

'We'd like to meet her. Does dinner on Saturday night suit you?'

'I'll check with Alina.'

'We'll look forward to seeing you. Goodbye, Ethan.'

He stood in front of the elevator, staring at his mobile, his gut twisting in regret. He had more cordial conversations with the people he spoke to regarding aspects of renovation or trading with his hotels. Was he destined to be as impersonal as his parents, considering he had their combined DNA?

The idea appalled.

He stabbed at his floor number, tapped his thigh on the journey up and strode purposely to the door. Alina came through from the lounge as he dropped his briefcase on the floor. His mind registered her sweet smile in the same instant as he wrapped her in his arms, burying his face into her silken curls, breathing in their citrus aroma. He relished her warmth, her softness, the way she stood still in his embrace, her only movement being to slide her arms around his waist.

Seconds ticked by. Holding her wasn't enough. He lifted his head. 'Hi.'

Their kiss was gentle, a mutual giving and taking. So soul-soothing he kept it short rather than risk pushing for more. This was new—something to build on. She was beginning to trust him as a man. He was beginning to reassess who he was.

She leant back in his arms to study his face.

'You caught up?'

Warmth radiated through him. This felt *right*. This was the way homecoming should always be. 'As good as. How did you go?'

'Two outfits which I love. One's here, the other needed some alteration, so I'll pick it up on Friday.'

'Only two?' He grinned down at the face she

pulled and kissed the tip of her nose. 'Whatever you feel comfortable with, Alina.'

'The new season stock's arriving in a week or two. By then I'll be bigger. Common sense says to buy what I need as I need it.'

His laughter shook his body. 'Since when did common sense become aligned with fashion shopping?'

'Hey!' She swatted his arm playfully, then froze as she realised what she'd done, eyes widening in shock.

Alina couldn't believe what she'd done. One second he'd been teasing her, the next she'd reciprocated. Completely spontaneously. Without thinking, she'd hit him, as if they'd been friends for a long time. The incredulous look on his face made it worse.

'I...' She tried to break free, suddenly found herself being lifted and carried backwards, to be plonked unceremoniously on the kitchen island. His hands gripped the bench either side of her. His impassive features gave no indication of his thinking. It was like their first meeting, but without the angst filling the room.

'Ethan, I—'

'Alina Fletcher,' he cut in. 'I do believe you are

starting to let your true self sneak out from its constrictions.'

She dropped her head. He lifted it with his finger, his thumb grazing her skin. His eyes sparkled with amusement, daring her to act again. The very fact that she wanted to scared her, holding her back. She trembled, held her breath. Then, as if of its own accord, her hand lifted, her fingers covering his on her chin.

The air around them seemed hot and heavy. She couldn't think straight His eyes darkened. His lips curled. Did his body sway closer? Did hers?

He abruptly withdrew his hand, pushing himself upright, shaking his head. 'A cool dip in the pool before dinner?'

Her body flopped. Gratefully, she seized on his suggestion. 'Yes. *Yes.*'

'Don't sound so eager to run, my sweet.' He swung her to the floor, keeping hold for a moment. 'And don't be afraid to show the woman you really are. I like what I've seen so far.'

Not trusting her voice, she gave a quick nod before turning away.

He stopped her with a gentle hand on her arm. 'My father's invited us to dinner on Saturday. I'm so angry with my mother I'm inclined to say no.'

'Delaying the inevitable? I think I'd rather face it now.'

'The way you did with me? I won't let them demean you, Alina.' A softly spoken declaration that demanded compliance. A firm hold she didn't want to break. Commanding blue eyes that enthralled.

'*You* were receptive,' she said. 'They're bound to think I'm trapping you. You're not the type to lose control and forget protection.'

Ethan never had. Even in his testosterone-driven teens he'd always been disciplined. Now, being with Alina every night, inhaling her essence, having her within easy reach, he appreciated how overpowering desire could be.

Anger ground in his gut. At his parents, who judged everyone by high, rigid standards and dismissed any contrary opinions. At himself for allowing them to influence his life, his behaviour. At the fates who had taken his sister's life when the best times were just beginning.

Yet those same fates had brought Alina and his future son or daughter to Sydney. To *him*.

Taking a short step forward, he manoeuvred her into his arms. In the simple act of holding her and stroking her hair he found solace as he reassured her.

'That's all the more reason for us to convince them of the undeniable magnetism between us. If we show them we're happy they'll have to accept it.'

'*Are* you happy?' A muffled plea into his shirt.

He tilted her chin to gaze into lovely despondent eyes and swore silently. Didn't she realise how much her being here meant to him?

'How can I *not* be happy? You've given me the most precious gift I'll ever have. You are giving a part of Louise back to me. Her child. You had easier options, yet you came to me not knowing how I'd react. You *did* know how my parents would.'

She took a long, shuddering breath, drawing his eyes to her full pink mouth. His body vibrated in response. She had no concept of what she was doing to him. He wasn't sure himself.

'Can we go this week? I'd prefer less time to dwell on it.'

His mobile rang before he could answer her. He grimaced at the caller ID. 'I agree. I've got to take this, so I'll meet you in the pool.'

He walked to his room, trying to focus on building regulations instead of smoky violet eyes and full, inviting lips.

Alina walked away, didn't look back. His words

had woven a soothing path through her mind, into her heart. Diminishing her qualms.

You've given me the most precious gift.

So similar to the phrase she'd heard from Louise when those two blue lines had materialised on that vital stick. Validation that she'd made the right decision to contact him now rather than after the birth.

Seven minutes to six on a Thursday evening and his desk was clear. Ethan felt pumped at an achievement he determined would become more routine than not. He conceded that the new promotions, which would become official at midnight on Sunday, made it possible.

He stopped on the way home for handmade chocolates to celebrate. Trying to quell the rush of anticipation, he entered the apartment, silently chuckling at the sci-fi epic music coming from the speakers.

Alina was preparing dinner at the kitchen counter. His eyes drank in her brunette curls, her enticing curves—soon to be curvier. Alluring. Desirable. This attraction was unlike any he'd ever experienced. Because of the situation? Her condition? His unexpected paternity? None of them explained that initial gut-clench when the only knowledge he'd had of her was her name.

She continued working, oblivious to his presence. How near did he have to be before she sensed him?

She had. The moment he'd opened the front door. Trying to quell her quickening heartbeat and ignore the prickling at the back of her neck was a futile exercise. There was nothing to account for her sudden heat rush.

Darn hormones. Why pick *this* pregnancy to play up? The first time—she couldn't prevent the comparisons surfacing—there'd been occasional morning sickness, a few cravings, and manageable backache in the last trimester. She'd been blissfully content, cherished, and pampered by...

She gripped the vegetable peeler till it stung, fought the tears threatening to spill.

His cologne seeped around her. Still no sound or greeting. Was he playing games, waiting for her to acknowledge him? She put down the peeler, pivoted.

Her lungs seized up. Her mouth dried. She sucked in her cheeks and swallowed, trying unsuccessfully to form moisture. Ethan stood there, gazing at her as if she were priceless, unique. When he walked round the island, smiling at her, she couldn't have moved if someone had tossed a grenade.

'You were so engrossed I didn't want to disturb you.' He cupped her chin, restarting her lungs in a short sharp gasp. He drew her to him as if their future was limitless and she leant into him, wanting to be closer. Wanting whatever he was offering.

He kissed her lightly, then deeper when her lips moved under his. When they parted of their own accord he accepted the tacit invitation. The tip of his tongue found hers. Heat flooded every cell. She tasted a hint of wine, coffee, tightened her hold on his neck, hungry for more.

Her stomach lurched. She wrenched free, clapping her hand over her mouth. Holding an arm across her belly, she bent double, trying not to throw up.

'Alina, what's wrong?'

The anxiety in his tone penetrated her brain. The support of his strong arms steadied her.

'Alina?'

The nausea hit again. Breaking free, she stumbled to the bathroom, crumpled beside the toilet bowl and dry-retched repeatedly. Didn't have time to worry about privacy.

CHAPTER TWELVE

WATER SPLASHED IN the basin and then Ethan was kneeling beside her, offering a damp cloth. She pressed it to her skin, letting the coolness soothe the heat from her humiliation. He'd kissed her and she'd practically thrown up on him.

Why? She'd eaten nothing, done nothing to trigger it. She shivered, couldn't stop, couldn't stem the shame churning in her belly.

'Alina?'

She looked up into blue eyes dark with concern. For the child? A tiny pang of regret hit her heart.

'I'm sorry, Ethan—so sorry. I've no idea what triggered that.'

He gently removed the cloth, tossed it into the sink, then cradled her to his chest.

'Hey, I've got friends with children. Over the years I've heard plenty of stories about so-called morning sickness. Including the fact that it should be named any-time-anywhere-for-no-apparent-reason sickness. Feeling better?'

She touched the stubble on his chin, managed a rueful half-smile. 'I think so.'

He helped her up, waited until she'd rinsed her mouth, then aided her walk back to the lounge. Sat beside her, his arm around her shoulders.

'Do you want some chocolate to take away the taste? I brought a box home.'

'Peppermint tea with plain biscuits will be more settling. I can get them.'

'You stay put. You're sure you're all right?'

For his sake she nodded, forcing a smile.

His eyes narrowed as if he wasn't convinced. 'My book contains a whole chapter on morning sickness, and its triggers. I think I'd better reread it.'

She put her hand on his thigh. 'Thank you for… for being there.'

'Always.' He kissed the top of her head. 'I'll be right back.'

Ethan went to the kitchen, turned on the kettle and sank against the bench, taut hands rubbing his face. He'd had to fight for composure in the bathroom; he still shook inside.

Seeing her sickly pallor as she'd hunched over the toilet had scared the hell out of him. Hearing the rasp in her voice had affected him in a way nothing had before. Because he'd feared for their baby? Or because Alina had been hurting? Both had ripped him apart.

On his return, he felt the taut knot in his gut ease at the tinge of colour in her cheeks. He gave her the tea and biscuits, scrutinised her as he drank his tea, the same flavour. If he had to he'd make herb tea his regular drink at home. Just in case.

'I feel better. Thank you.' She started to rise.

He stopped her, catching hold of her arm. 'You're sure?'

Her smile was steadier. 'I'm fine.'

Alina went to the kitchen, where the salad she'd been preparing waited, not realising he was behind her until he spoke.

'What can I do to help?'

Help? He hadn't offered before. She'd never been sick before. 'I can manage. You go do whatever you had planned.'

He hesitated, his cobalt eyes gleaming with an emotion she didn't dare try to decipher. The new upheaval in her abdomen had nothing to do with her being pregnant.

'Go. I can handle kebabs and salad.'

Why did it take so much effort to drag her eyes

from him? She forced herself to concentrate on the half-finished carrot.

'I'll call you when it's ready.'

The grunt he made was unintelligible and utterly male. It tickled the edge of her memory. Was quickly relegated to the clouds, where it belonged. She sneaked a peek as he left, wished she hadn't.

His grey shirt was moulded to muscles toned to perfection from swimming and working out. Her gaze was drawn down past his trim waist to firm buttocks that flexed with each step. Her breath quickened. This was crazy. She was checking him out like a teenager.

Her knees shook. She flattened her hands on the benchtop for support, barely aware of the peeler handle digging into her palm. She craved ice-cold water, cursed the heat flooding her body. Daren't risk walking to the tap.

He spun round, catching her off guard. 'By the way…' His mouth stayed open. His eyes widened. He grinned—a conspiratorial I-know-what-you're-thinking grin. Moved slowly towards her, holding her spellbound with captivating blue eyes.

The music from the speakers reached a dramatic crescendo, heightening the atmosphere. It had hardly registered until then. Now it filled the space between them. The width of the room. The breadth of the kitchen island. The length of his arm.

She faced him, her brain in a quandary as warnings of danger sparred with reminders of his kisses. He halted at that arm's distance, his eyes now sombre, his features composed. A façade. She noted his rigid stance, the way he'd fisted his hands.

'Are you game to try again?'

She heard the caution in his voice. The kiss? He'd initiated it; she was the one who'd allowed it to become more intimate. This time there'd be no intoxicating flavour of wine or coffee. She guessed he'd used mouthwash, had seen him drink peppermint tea. Just in case.

Until Tuesday's highly emotional embrace in the pool his kisses had been mostly tender—a gentle way of gradually familiarising her with his touch. Their intimate kiss, though interrupted, had been a giant advance in their relationship. A definite declaration that he found her attractive. Desired her.

There'd been no mention of their sleeping together, but she couldn't deny her body responded to his virility, couldn't stop his image invading her thoughts. Oh, Lord, had her nausea been triggered by guilt, by feelings of infidelity?

He quietly waited for her answer. They both knew there was only one way to resolve the issue.

'Yes.'

Her single husky word had him enfolding her and gently covering her mouth with his. The music faded. The air around them crackled. Time stood still. His lips moved slowly, persuasively over hers. His hands stroked unhurriedly, without pressure. He kept space between their bodies.

Her fingertips inched up his chest until they touched his skin. His body trembled. His earthy Ethan aroma filled her lungs, clouding her brain. Dominating her will. Freeing her will. Her fingers twisted into his hair. Her lips parted.

Ethan held his breath, every muscle tensed in a supreme effort not to sweep his tongue inside to explore the sweetness he'd sampled earlier. Being restrained with a woman was a new experience for him. Mutual attraction led to equally satisfying sex. No strings. No commitment.

This was different. For indefinable reasons. After the initial spontaneous jolt everything he'd done had been influenced by the fact she was pregnant.

Or had it? When they were apart she was in his head. When they were together he couldn't stop looking, touching and inhaling her essence, fresh as spring.

He slowly traced a line with his tongue around the soft, moist inside of her lips. She gasped, taking in his breath. Quivered under his roaming hands. His body hardened and he shuffled his feet, widening the gap. Sliding his tongue in deeper, he cautiously stoked hers, fully prepared to stop at the slightest hint of distress.

There was none—only a timid response that almost had him hauling her closer. There was no sense of time. It felt as if he were standing on the edge of a precipice, knowing there was something wonderful waiting if he'd just let himself fall. With a rough shuddering breath he lifted his head to gaze into clear, shining eyes.

'I guess it was one of those inexplicable pregnancy things, huh?'

Her spontaneous laugh zapped his already strained senses.

'Seems like it.'

To double-check, he kissed her briefly, firmly. 'So—you feel okay?' His pulse kicked up even higher when she flick-licked her bottom lip and smiled, as if she'd tasted something delicious.

'Go—or you won't be eating dinner tonight.'

He went, deeming it an option he'd happily choose.

On Saturday morning Alina paced restlessly round the apartment. Something was itching at her brain—wouldn't surface, wouldn't go. She'd booted up her computer. Closed it down. She'd changed, walked into the gym, turned, walked out. Changed back into jeans and a top. Curled up with her embroidery, packed it away after a few stitches. Every room was tidy; everything was clean.

She glanced at the kitchen calendar and the notation for tonight: *Dinner with parents.* An unavoidable ordeal to be endured. She was convinced they wouldn't be adding her to their regular guest list unless they wanted Ethan there too. And he'd given her the impression he'd happily miss most of their organised events.

A picture flashed into her head at the sight of today's date. She quickly blocked it out. She didn't do special days.

Tenuous, ghost-like memories nipped at the edge of her mind, wouldn't be dismissed. Tears welled in her eyes as memories crashed back. Her mother-in-law's birthday. *Mum*. Unlike Sophia, she'd welcomed Alina, drawn her into the family and loved her as a daughter. She'd be lucky if Sophia tolerated her for the time she was here.

Ethan had family and friends for support. She didn't begrudge him any of them; he'd need all the help available next year. She had no one. Unless…

You only have to reach out. There'll be no recriminations, only love and understanding.

Her thumb trembled as she scrolled through her phone for the name and number. A short tear-choked conversation later she grabbed her handbag and ran out the door, heading for the one person she could tell anything. Though she wouldn't reveal the whole truth.

Where was she? Ethan drummed his fingers on his office desk, forced himself to focus on the computer screen, rereading figures he hadn't taken in before. They were good. His mindset wasn't. He exited the program, scowling. Why hadn't she returned his calls?

He hadn't been concerned when she hadn't answered her mobile or the apartment phone at first, assuming she was in the gym area. Now, however… He checked his watch for the umpteenth time. Ten past twelve—over two hours since his first call.

He rotated sideways, staring at the city skyline, seeing only her face, wondering why she'd been so subdued this morning after they'd spent two enjoyable evenings together. Maybe it was one of the mood swings detailed in his book.

He grabbed his phone again, hesitated with his hand in mid-air. It rang, vibrating in his palm. Wrong caller ID. After quickly dealing with the matter, he went to the coffee machine. With re-filled mug in hand he paced the floor, trying to convince himself it was normal trepidation given her condition.

In truth, she'd triggered something inside him from the moment they'd met—something incomprehensible. She didn't fit his long-term plan in any way. Grieving and haunted, she was determined not to stay in Australia. He wouldn't stop her leaving, though he'd give her support for as long as she wished. He wasn't perfect, but the child she carried needed a parent as hang-up-free as possible. And right now *he* needed her to answer her damn phone.

Grabbing a printed report on his Gold Coast hotel, he sprawled on the long sofa, his mug and mobile on the low table by his side. Normally he'd have been elated that the renovations were on schedule and under budget.

Startled by his ringtone, he almost knocked over his coffee in his haste to grab his phone. His adrenaline spiked when he saw the caller ID. He sucked in air, tried to project a calm he definitely didn't feel.

'Alina.'

'Ethan, I'm sorry.'

Her distressed voice chilled his heart. Feigned calm flew out of the window. He was on his feet, striding to grab his jacket as he spoke.

'What's wrong? Where are you? I'll come for you.' Hell, he felt as desperate as he sounded.

'No! It's nothing. I'm an idiot, that's all.' Breathless. Anxious.

He stilled. Wished he was there so he could see her face, read how upset she really was. 'Tell me.'

'I went to visit my husband's aunt. We sat in the garden and my bag was inside, on her sofa. I missed all your calls.'

Spontaneous laughter surged up his throat and burst out at the simple explanation. She was all right. She was safe. He perched on his desk, torn between pure relief and self-reproach for worrying so much.

'It's not funny. I've got six messages from you.'

Her slightly miffed tone was endearing.

'I'm just glad you're okay. Where are you now?'

'Sitting on a bus.'

He wanted her here, wanted to hold her. Wanted to shake her for scaring him. Kiss her until she melted in his arms.

'Why were you calling?' she added.

'My father rang, asking if we could arrive half an hour earlier tonight.'

She was always ready on time—he could have called when he left the office. Then he wouldn't have had two hours of angst. Or heard her sweet, apologetic voice.

'No last-minute reprieve, huh?'

'I'm afraid not. You're sure you're okay?' He sure as hell hadn't been, two minutes ago.

'I'm fine. I'm truly sorry for worrying you, Ethan.'

'Worrying me? You, my sweet, are putting me through emotions I can't even name.'

He ended the call, huffing the air from his lungs as he tossed his phone onto his desk. He wasn't normally prone to panic. If there was a problem he coolly and methodically searched for a solution.

Was this new apprehension going to be part of his future? A normality of being a parent? He'd probably be overloaded with advice and disaster stories once his friends found out about his impending fatherhood. Knowing they'd be there for him and his child, he'd take it all in the spirit it would be given.

Alina had said she had no family, and yet there was this aunt—her husband's aunt. And maybe other relatives? How close was she to them? Close enough to want to re-establish contact. Why deny them before? Why turn to them now?

Hell, he'd hardly learnt anything about her; she kept her guard up tight. That hadn't been an issue when they'd met and agreed to marry for the child's sake. Now she was real to him, she was special in a way he'd never felt before. *He* wanted to be the one she reached out to for support.

Alina wriggled uneasily on the bus seat. Unflappable, down-to-earth Ethan had been rattled until she'd explained. If that teenager texting with his head bent hadn't bumped into her, she wouldn't have thought to check her phone. An incident she'd skip mentioning. She accepted his reasons for being over-protective, preferred not to give him cause to be more so.

She replayed his words in her mind. He'd seemed genuinely concerned for her. The tenderness in his voice during that last remark had almost had her saying, *Ditto*.

Once he'd recovered from the initial shock of her pregnancy he'd been very supportive. He hadn't pressured her for the details of her life she'd rather keep private. And, while his physical attraction to her was obvious, his manner had been concilia-tory, letting her set the boundaries.

It was parent confrontation time. Ethan glanced at the dashboard clock and eased his foot on the ac-celerator. Alina sat quietly, hadn't said much at all since he'd arrived home. There'd only been time for him to grab a quick shower and change before leaving. He'd still had the reality of her having rel-atives on his mind, hadn't wanted to talk either. Even if he could figure out how to bring up the subject, now was not the time.

He glanced over. She was staring ahead, pale and rigid, as if being driven to the guillotine. Her left hand was hidden but he'd bet it was doing that finger dance. His heart wrenched. Sweet, brave Alina, with demons he could only imagine, was prepared to confront his ultra-judgemental parents for *his* benefit, and he was jealous because she'd called someone who'd be on her side.

Jealous! No, he couldn't be. He flicked her another look, felt a deep surge of tenderness. Accepted the reality of that emotion, new for him.

Taking his hand from the wheel, he gently covered hers for a few seconds. 'You are beautiful, Alina Fletcher. I'm proud to have you by my side— any time, anywhere.'

His reward was a tentative smile. He wanted more.

Alina toyed with her hair, smoothed her skirt over her slightly rounded belly. Was it too late to ask him to take her home? Too late. Too cowardly. They were the child's nearest relatives, next to him. Maybe they'd mellow with age; grandparents often did. She'd be gone soon, so any adverse judgement on her shouldn't impact on Ethan or the baby.

The vibes she'd picked up from Ethan had exacerbated her tension, turning the butterflies in her tummy to turbulent judders. She wished she were anywhere else—like on the Manly Ferry, steaming across the heads, wind blowing her hair, spray cooling her cheeks. And Ethan surrounding her, his chest at her back, arms at her sides. Shielding her. Protective.

Her eyes widened and she pressed back in her seat as they drove through the gates of the formidable James couple's opulent home. It was a two-storey, luxurious mansion, like something out of a magazine, set in flawless landscaped gardens. The back area was as impressive as the front.

They pulled up. Reluctant to leave the security of the vehicle, she sat, vaguely aware of him moving around the front of the vehicle, opening her door and hunkering down beside her. Gentle fingers stroked her arm. Empathetic eyes met hers when she looked up.

'Remember, this is all for show. The house. The decor. Their attitude. Real life is you, me and our baby.'

His hand splayed protectively over her stomach, radiating warmth with his touch, diminishing her fears. A little.

'You won't be left alone with either of them. They can insinuate all they like; they'll only learn what we choose to tell them.'

Unbuckling her seatbelt, he helped her out. She

gripped his hand, felt his flesh dent under her nails. 'I'm worried I'll let you down.'

He shook his head. 'Impossible. You're the bravest woman I've ever met. Our marriage, our lives, are exactly that. *Ours.* Don't forget, it's they who are on notice.'

Giving her that special Ethan smile, he raised her hand and pressed his lips to her palm. Electrifying quivers sped along her veins, through her, settling in her stomach. A lovely, if slightly scary feeling. She smiled back and he led her round to the front steps. She was thankful her flowing dress hid her condition, grateful for the strength of his fingers entwined with hers.

CHAPTER THIRTEEN

ETHAN RANG THE DOORBELL, wishing they were home…alone. Alina's trembling vibrated through his palm and his heart twisted. Taking her into his arms, he kissed her for comfort, keeping it tender. Until he heard her contented sigh. Until she softened into him.

'Try to contain yourself, Ethan. There's no excuse for a public exhibition.'

Alina flinched. Ethan barely stirred at the caustic remark from behind him, though his gut tightened with irritation. Then he reluctantly lifted his head, scanning the large empty garden before grinning wryly.

'Hardly public, Father.'

His chest expanded as he smiled down at Alina, seeing her sweet blush and the glow in her eyes. *He'd* done that—taken her from apprehension to desire. With a kiss that contained a promise for later.

'Alina, this is my father—Martin James. Father, I'd like you to meet Alina Fletcher.'

His father inclined his head towards her. 'Please come in, Ms Fletcher.'

Embarrassment flooded Ethan at the stilted remark. He stiffened, quite prepared to walk away. Alina forestalled him, moving forward, hand extended. Leaving his father no choice but to accept her greeting.

'Thank you, Mr James. It's very kind of you and your wife to invite me.' Deliciously tongue in cheek.

The air whooshed from his lungs. He stared in admiration at this poised woman whom he'd sensed had been ready to bolt a few minutes ago. She'd been surprising him from the moment they met. Anticipation of the months ahead zipped along his veins.

They entered together, Alina's hand in his once more. Was she comparing the cold, immaculate decor to the welcoming, comfy atmosphere of Louise's courtyard home in Barcelona? He did—every time he came here.

A sharp intake of breath at his side made him aware he was crushing her fingers. He loosened his grip, gave her an apologetic glance—and was completely thrown when she winked her left eye at him. A simple act that triggered a fuzzy memory of something shared. Of concealed laughter.

Alina noticed his startled expression, but had no time to jog his memory. Sophia James was waiting for them. She lifted her chin, quite prepared to confront the woman who would one day take great pleasure in telling her son, *I told you so.*

He knew it, accepted it, and would handle it with his natural diplomacy. At least he'd have the consolation of his son or daughter.

Why the sudden depression? She'd asked for her freedom—had to have it. Had to keep moving. No ties. No commitments. Keep the memories blocked out. She feared there was now going to be so much more she'd have to not remember.

Sophia was standing regally, ready to be greeted. She reminded Alina of the titled women of history—so proud, so extremely conscious of their presumed status in life. With another quick squeeze of her hand Ethan led her forward, not letting go as he greeted his mother with a light kiss on her proffered cheek.

'Mother, you've already met Alina—though I understand it was a brief encounter.'

Alina hoped she was the only one who heard the

nuances in his introduction. Felt a flush of warmth at his championship.

'Yes, it was quite a surprise. Welcome, Alina.' Sophia gave her an obligatory social air-kiss on both cheeks. 'Shall we all sit for drinks?' She raised a perfectly trimmed eyebrow at Alina. 'Do you have a favourite cocktail, my dear?

'Iced water, thank you. I don't drink.'

Spoken so woodenly she didn't recognise her voice. She cringed inside at the pointed look exchanged between the older couple. This wasn't a family dinner; it was a formal... She didn't know what it was.

She *did* know she had the support of the man whose firm hand now guided her to the deep-cushioned sofa. For as long as she stayed in Australia—maybe even longer. His innate integrity ensured that he'd never betray or disown her. Life would have been so much better if only this staid, society-obsessed couple had appreciated the genuine affable qualities of their children.

Ethan kept his arm around her, even after a pointed scowl from his father when he gave them their drinks. He now fully comprehended the primitive male urge to protect a mate. It reinforced his determination to have everyone believe that he had married for love.

'How is the Gold Coast hotel coming along, Ethan? Is the projected opening still viable?'

'Yes, Father, but I'd rather not talk business. This is family time. Mother, I hear the charity night at the opera house you helped organise was a great success?'

'Thank you, Ethan. I'd hoped to see you there.'

'Not my scene. To support your cause I did buy three double tickets, as a bonus for ardent followers at work.'

'Opera's an acquired taste. You never gave it a chance,' his father stated.

'Simone attended with her parents,' his mother chimed in. 'She was very gracious with her condolences, and apologised for missing Louise's funeral due to a modelling assignment in New York.'

Her voice slowed as Ethan's head jerked up. His brow furrowed as a powerful surge of emotion ripped through him. *Louise. The wink.*

He flicked a quick glance at Alina, whose gaze was focused on his mother.

His sister's favourite ploy as a child—and sometimes in adulthood—had been winking, always with the left eye, to defuse a tense situation. It was one that had so often had them squirming in their seats, trying not to laugh. Alina had deliberately given him a reminder of happy times.

'Simone is the daughter of friends, Alina. She and Ethan have been close for *years*. Now, tell us about yourself. Do you have a profession?' Sophia's words were syrup-sweet, politely phrased with a definite hint of disdain.

Alina met her condescending brown eyes full-on, thought of how Louise had suffered because of this woman's attitude, and remembered her happiness when the procedure had worked. In less than a heartbeat all her apprehension evaporated.

'No. I've never needed one. I speak three languages fluently; get by in a few others. Travelling through Europe has taught me more than I'd have learnt at any university. Hands-on life is a great teacher.'

'Oh, so how do you make a living?' Slightly more acidic.

'By accepting honest casual work in a variety of places and industries.'

She felt disapproval radiate through the room. Should she continue? She hated deceit, even when it was warranted or unavoidable. This wasn't.

'Barcelona was my base. That's where I became friends with Leon and Louise.'

'So that's where you two met? Ethan…' Sophia stopped talking, flashed a wary look at her son.

'Please continue, Mother.' Ethan's arm tightened around her shoulders. His flat, calm tone should have served as a warning. His mother missed it.

'I realise dealing with everything was paramount, but you never mentioned meeting anyone there. It hasn't even been two months since the accident, and she's…'

Another hesitation. Alina guessed it was very unusual for this very outspoken woman.

'She's what?' Harsher. A definite signal to back off.

'Oh, come on, Ethan. What do you expect?' Martin James obviously couldn't contain himself. 'You chose not to tell us about her, when you met or how. She's obviously led a nomadic life, with no ties or responsibilities. Now she's moved in with you. I assume she's not working?'

Alina's heart pounded; her stomach heaved. She heard the words, understood the implications but not the undertones. They seemed to be talking of someone or something else, using her as the target. She'd been prepared for personal questions or subtle jibes—not this blatant hostility.

No one had ever treated her this way—as if she weren't good enough to be in their company. Swinging her head from wife to husband, she saw only harsh dissatisfaction. She wanted out. She turned to Ethan—and froze.

Cold chills swept over her as she recalled his pained features after he'd read the surrogacy documents, his fury when she'd suggested his family might not want the baby. Right now he was rigidly controlled, icy. Much more intimidating.

Ethan had never been angrier. Not when a trusted friend had betrayed his loyalty. Not when a long-time girlfriend had cheated on him. Not even when a stupid, avoidable thing like a faulty brake had taken his sister and his best friend from him.

The rage building inside him was a culmination of years of their haranguing him to conform to their views, virulent criticism of his own choices. Their deplorable treatment of Leon and Louise. Plus a deep conviction that defending Alina was paramount—above anything he had ever done. Or ever would.

He rose to his feet, taking her with him, acutely aware that his teeth had ground together and his free hand had balled into a fist. One glance at Alina's face and his only thought was to get out of there, so he could beg her forgiveness for subjecting her to this poisonous atmosphere.

'This charade is over.'

'Ethan, we—'

He flicked his hand, silencing his mother, dismissing both parents. Tenderly brushing a curl from Alina's brow, he kissed her forehead. 'Let's go home, darling.'

He turned his head as they reached the door, subliminally noting their gobsmacked expressions.

'Stay away from our home. Any calls will not be answered or returned.'

The son who'd always been the mediator had finally rebelled.

Ethan refrained from gunning his car as they left the property. The fierce urge to put distance between him and his parents was tempered by the knowledge that he had the most precious cargo.

He had no doubt they'd blame Alina, having always previously claimed to their friends that it was business commitments that had caused his withdrawal from their social world. *Damn. Idiot.* He ought to have insisted their first meeting be held in a restaurant, where they'd have had no choice but to be socially polite.

Probably wouldn't have changed the end result.

He glanced across, met wounded eyes in an ash-white face and hit the brake, swinging into the kerb. He flung off his seatbelt, hauling Alina into his arms as he fumbled for her clasp. Holding her against his heart, breathing in her subtle aroma, was so liberating after the overpowering room they'd left behind, his anger began to dissipate.

'I needed this. Needed your sweetness.' He stroked her back, brushed her hair with his lips. 'I'm sorry, Alina—forgive me for taking you there. You've done nothing to deserve the way they treated you. Nothing.'

She gave a muted sound suspiciously like a sob into his chest. He threaded his fingers thorough her hair and tilted her head up. Wanted to wipe the deep sorrow in her eyes away for ever. Hated that he didn't know how. Her trembling lips broke his heart.

'Why are they like that? No one's ever treated me as if I'm nothing, not good enough to be polite to. *No one*—in all the places I've been.'

'And they'll never get another chance.'

'No.' She pushed away, shaking her head.

'They're your parents, Ethan, your family. Don't lock the door. Life can change in a split second and then it's too late to go back. We both know that.'

He threw his head back against his seat, closed his eyes. He did know, and it hurt like hell. Her self-deprecating laugh penetrated the anguish.

'I think, somewhere deep in my head, I expected them to accept me the way Colin's parents did.'

His eyes flew open at the mention of her husband. She sat, half turned towards him, hands in her lap, eyes downcast. He held his breath, didn't dare move a muscle.

'We met when he was twenty, still at uni. I was only seventeen, and a major distraction to his studies, yet his parents welcomed me, treating me like a loved daughter. They were so thrilled when...'

Lord, it was so hard not to reach for her as she painfully struggled for the next word.

'When M... M... Michael was born. We were a real family.'

She went silent. Seemed immobile. Waiting was excruciating, but he sensed there was more she wanted to say. For her own sake.

'They're all gone. I'm not.' Her head came up, eyes big and dark with despair. 'Why just me?' She began to tremble violently.

Now he moved, spurred by the stabbing pain that raked him. He enfolded her into his warmth. Desperate to comfort her, desperate for comfort himself. She'd been the only survivor. She might have died too.

Headlights lit up the windscreen. Alina pulled back, blinking, trying to regain composure. She hadn't spoken about the accident since it had happened. Why now? Why to Ethan?

'Take me home. Please.'

He didn't move, kept a loose hold on her, his features grey and heartrending, his eyes dark and tortured.

'Ethan?'

His shoulders shook as he shuddered. His eyes refocused.

'Home. Yes, let's go home.'

When they arrived at the apartment Alina stayed Ethan's hand when he reached for the light switch.

'Leave them off.'

The lights from the city gave the room a soft glow, a more confiding atmosphere. He'd defended her against his parents' insinuations; he deserved to know more than the half-reveal she'd given him.

At least the meagre details she hadn't been able to avoid learning.

She poured herself a glass of water, and took her defensive place on the settee. Ethan followed with a cold beer—the drink he usually favoured in afternoons. When he saw the way she was huddled in the corner his brow furrowed, but he chose the other end, folding one leg up, his body towards her.

She drank half the glass to clear her throat, then fixed her gaze on the window. There was no emotion in her flat, detached voice.

'We'd been on a week's holiday, touring places near the New South Wales and Victoria border. The plan was to stop for the night, then drive home. Colin and his dad were both careful drivers, changing over whenever we stopped. It was getting dark, and I heard them talk of the next town being about thirty minutes away before I fell asleep.'

Ethan gripped the cold metal can so hard it began to buckle. His throat was so tight he could hardly breathe. He knew what was coming, didn't want to hear it. Couldn't avoid it. Couldn't take his eyes from her pale, impassive face and blank, unseeing eyes. He watched her drain her glass, swallow with difficulty, and shiver as she drew in breath.

'Everything's a blur after that. Screams, thuds, screeching metal. Voices and sirens. That hospital smell. I don't remember who told me. Someone in the corridor mentioned a kangaroo and a semitrailer. I didn't want to know—never want to know.' Her voice broke. 'I had concussion from a head wound, lots of cuts and bruises. And they all died.'

Her empty glass fell into her lap. She hunched over, covering her face with her hands.

Ethan's hand shook as he put down his drink and automatically moved her glass to the table. Her words had torn an agonising path into the depths of his soul. A tiny twist of fate and he'd never have known her.

Would she push him away if he reached for her? His confidence faltered.

'Alina?' Desperate. Begging to help her. 'I'm here. Whenever you want or need me.'

She lifted tortured eyes that stared at him as if she wondered who he was, why he was there. Then her face cleared and she flung herself into his arms.

'Ethan. Hold me.'

He cradled her as close as humanly possible, needing to reassure her. Needing reassurance himself. *She was meant to live. Meant to have this baby with him. Meant to love again one day.*

'Hold me tight, Ethan. Hold me. Please don't let me be alone.'

He held her. For as long as she'd let him, he'd hold her.

'You're not alone any more, darling. I'm not going anywhere. Not without you. I'll be here to hold you, comfort and care for you. You, my beautiful, courageous Alina.'

He caressed her back, murmured words from his heart, knowing she might not understand. Knowing only that he needed to voice how much she'd come to mean to him. The baby she carried was an added joy.

He kept talking, even after her body softened in sleep against him. He had no idea when she'd be ready to hear his admission in the cold light of day.

A long-forgotten sensation infiltrated Alina's brain, enticing her to wake; less pleasant ones held her in limbo. A familiar earthy aroma surrounded her. A light breeze stirred her hair. She moved, yet the warm wall at her side stayed. Warmth spread from the weight on her stomach.

Her senses kicked in. Her eyes fluttered, flew

open. She was lying on her back, early-morning light allowing her to see an unknown painting on the wrong wall. A white-sleeve-covered arm stretched out from under her neck. She was in Ethan's arms. In his bed. Still wearing her dress.

Her last recollection was of Ethan twisting them both so they lay prone on the settee, of his hands soothing her to sleep. He'd done as she'd pleaded, had cradled her. Hadn't left her on her own.

She turned her head. He lay on his side, his chest moving in steady rhythm. Hassle-free in sleep, his features were softer, the tiny lines at the corners of his eyes less obvious. His stubbled jaw was strangely appealing. He slept so peacefully for a man whose world had been blown apart. By her.

She arched her neck. To wake the sleeping Prince with a kiss? Crazy notion. She rolled towards the edge of the bed.

'Alina?' Slumber-rough and drowsy.

His hand caught her arm, slipped off, and she slid onto the floor.

'It's late. I have things to do.'

Like run from an awkward situation.

CHAPTER FOURTEEN

ETHAN HAD THE table set when Alina arrived in the dining area, calm and guarded. She quickly sat down without speaking, not giving him the chance to be polite. He understood her reticence, hoped she'd still feel able to talk about her family.

She flicked a glance at him as he put a mug of peach tea in front of her. A delicate rosy hue coloured her skin. Where was the feistiness she'd shown in the past?

He felt her gaze follow him as he took his seat, grabbed his favourite cereal and filled his bowl.

'That was cowardly of me.'

Subdued tone. Why was she so nervous? Waiting for her to elucidate, he prayed her confession hadn't caused a regression in their growing relationship.

'When I woke up in your bed I bolted like a naive teenager.'

He nodded. 'A natural reaction after your revelations, Alina.'

She filled her bowl with fruity nut muesli, kept her head down while she ate, as if mulling over an important issue.

'Was there a woman in your life when I came?'

He spluttered on his coffee. Hell, she kept finding new ways to surprise him.

'There hasn't been anyone for a long time. I swear there will be no one as long as you are with me.'

Her nod was barely perceptible. She swallowed as she averted her gaze, reinforcing her apprehension. Hidden under the table, her left hand would be performing its ritual dance.

'Do… Do you expect… Want me to move into your room after the wedding?'

She completely took his breath away with that one. His jaw dropped; adrenaline zapped through his veins. He'd been trying to work out how to introduce the topic gently; she'd come right out with it. He leant back, studying her, wondering if she realised how courageous and strong she was.

'Alina Fletcher, you are amazing. I've bulldozed you into agreements you'd rather run a mile from. My actions have rekindled harrowing memories you'd prefer were left buried. Yet you offer compromises which will reinforce our child's parentage.'

Her eyes widened as he spoke. The soft blush he'd begun to anticipate and adore tinged her cheeks. Across the table was too far a distance. Pushing his chair away, he walked around it, took her hand and lifted her to her feet. Cupped her cheek.

'Having you in my arms as I fell asleep felt better than anything I can remember. As if protecting you and our baby gives my life true meaning for the first time. I'd like to feel that way every night, but the choice is yours, Alina. Now, after we're married or never. I want you there only if it's where *you* want to be.'

She placed her hand over his heart, her lips curling into a sweet smile and a warm glow flickering in her eyes.

'It felt nice.' She glanced away, breathed in, then met his eyes again. 'Can we talk about Colin's aunt and uncle? Jean and Ray?'

Any subject was fine by him. Every conversation revealed a little more of who they were and brought them closer. He settled her back into her seat.

Alina gathered the thoughts that had tumbled through her mind as she'd showered and dressed.

Looking into Ethan's sympathetic eyes, she suddenly found it easy.

'They were the ones who held it all together for me after… Well, you know. They and the solicitor arranged everything—cleared the house and sold it, put everything in storage.'

She stopped, turned her head to stare at the floor. Looked at him again.

'They took me in and cared for me, even though they were grieving too. I owed them so much and I ran. Fled the country. I phoned or wrote occasionally, and sent postcards of the places I visited. Yesterday she was so welcoming…refused to let me feel guilty.'

'Because she understands. You needed time and distance to heal. I'd like to meet them. And I think you'd like them to be at our wedding.'

'Yes, very much.'

'After we've eaten, ring and see if they're home today.

Unlucky to see the bride before the wedding? *Yeah, right—that had really worked for her before.*

Sophia James had probably insisted that Louise follow tradition. And Alina hadn't been able to

deny Jean's request after she'd been so supportive, even promising to keep the wedding a secret.

Ethan had won Jean and Ray over with his charm
and sincerity, convincing them that Alina was the
only woman he'd ever wanted to marry. Jean truly
believed he loved her. Only Alina knew he wanted
to ensure the baby's right to his name.

After a teasing protest he had agreed to let Alina
and Jean spend two nights in the hotel suite in
order to shop and prepare. His compromise had
been being allowed to have a short time alone with
Alina the night before the ceremony.

He'd sat beside her in the lounge, took her hand
and pressed his lips to her knuckles.

'Everything had to be arranged so quickly we
didn't follow many of the usual traditions. This
one I can make right.'

Before she could speak he stunned her by dropping to one knee without relinquishing his hold.

'Alina Fletcher, will you marry me tomorrow?
Be my wife for as long as you feel you can?'

Her heart lurched at the hitch in his voice on
the second question. Her eyes misted; her throat
choked up. She looked into sincere cobalt eyes and
her answer came easily.

'Yes, I'll marry you, Ethan.' She refused to think about the time limit right now.

He pulled a flat black box engraved with a familiar jeweller's name from his jacket. The exquisite amethyst pendant was a flawless match for her engagement ring. Another thoughtful gift she wasn't sure she deserved.

She stared wide-eyed at this man who'd so drastically changed her life, pushed and cajoled her in matters he deemed important, eased off and given her freedom in others. Like where she slept. Knowing she was attracted to him, yet still unsure of herself, she hadn't slept with him again. As promised, he hadn't mentioned it.

Over the last two weeks they'd slipped into an easy friendship she wanted to maintain though it was inexplicably frustrating sometimes. Hormones again?

'It's lovely, Ethan. Why...?'

'Because I wanted to.'

His lips covered hers in a long tender kiss. She slid the box onto the couch, leant in and wound her arms around his neck. Somehow she ended up in his lap on the floor, wishing he could stay.

When he left his whispered, 'I'll miss you...' was as tender as his kiss.

* * *

The wedding party was waiting for them in the roof garden. She had no reason to stall. Her hair shone with new highlights, its longer length framing her face and curling on her neck. The make-up applied by a beautician was light and perfect. Her long chiffon dress, shimmering with shades of lilac and silver, fell softly over her burgeoning bump. Her new necklace completed the illusion.

This wasn't the shy girl in a white princess gown who had trembled with eager anticipation eleven years ago. The woman staring at her today was a mature stranger, fulfilling a vow to friends. No wildly beating heart. No dreams of eternal love. Strip off the trappings and tonight's ceremony was just a formal recognition of the decision Ethan had made to remedy a family dilemma.

Everything changed the moment she stepped out of the elevator. He was watching for her, impeccably dressed in a dark suit, white shirt and dark blue tie, his brilliant cobalt gaze immediately zoning in on hers. A dashing knight waiting for his princess.

Her feet refused to move forward. Sensations cascaded through her brain, impossible to separate. Except for the one certainty she'd clung to since consenting to his scheme—her trust in this man, and her absolute belief that he'd never hurt or betray her.

Her palms began to sweat as they gripped her orchid and fern bouquet. Her insides melted in a rush of heat while her heartbeat crashed into a rock 'n' roll drum rhythm.

A gentle nudge came from behind her. 'He's waiting for you, Alina.'

Not any more. He strode forward, eyes gleaming, his radiant smile just for her. Taking her hands, he drew her to him, the rough timbre of his voice revealing his emotion. 'Exquisite. Unforgettable.'

Through misty eyes she was vaguely aware of Jean moving past her to join the others, glimpsed a photographer beside the celebrant. The city noises faded until there was only Ethan holding her, surrounded by a neon-enhanced darkening blue sky.

His lips touched hers lightly, reverently. In an instant her mind cleared. Her reservations dissipated. She kissed him back, standing on tiptoe for deeper contact. The tremor that shook his body echoed in hers. They walked together to the flower festooned arch where she relinquished her bouquet, allowing them to join hands as they stood face to face.

At this service the male response was calmer, clearer than the one so long ago. It ought to be impassive. Yet there was something in the resonance of his voice, in the pressure of his grasp and in the depths of his eyes that chipped at the barricades guarding her heart. She replied with the vows that would bind her to him in kind, without qualms or hesitation.

'I pronounce you husband and wife.'

Not waiting for permission, Ethan kissed her with all the fervour of a loving groom. Hugs and kisses were exchanged, and after the certificates were signed they all moved to a small lamplit marquee.

The first toast was to the bride and groom, wishing them a long and happy life together. As they clinked glasses Ethan's piercing eyes sent a message for her alone. His distinct, 'To us!' triggered a pleasurable shiver.

The celebrant left and then their entrées were served. The wine waiter refilled their glasses and moved discreetly away.

Ethan spoke next. 'To those who will always be remembered, living on in our hearts.' He held out his glass to Alina, dropped his gaze to her stomach and mouthed *Louise and Leon*. She reciprocated, touching her glass to his.

Then *her husband*—a phrase she'd believed

she'd never think or say again—surprised her even more. His fingertips gently lifted her chin and his eyes darkened with intensity as he repeated the salute. Her eyes misted as she understood his generous gesture. For Colin, his parents and Michael.

The sweet liquid caught in her throat as she suddenly realised there'd been only a numbing sorrow as she'd thought their names. Had she come through the darkness, as Jean had suggested this morning? Not really. Ethan found it so easy to believe in *our* baby. Her maternal feelings had died on a dusky country road.

She was definitely appreciative of the delicious specially prepared courses, making a mental note to send a written thank-you to the chef and his staff. Everyone in the know had been loyal and discreet—a tribute to the man by her side.

Ethan fiddled with his new gold ring. The sun had set. Hot drinks and handmade chocolates had been served. He was married—something he hadn't envisaged in his foreseeable future. If he ever had, he would have imagined his choice would be one of his peers—a successful woman with interests they'd share, who had no desire to procreate.

Circumstances and his code of honour had dictated otherwise. Yet to his amazement he felt satisfied, content, as if he'd found a unique treasure he hadn't realised he'd been searching for. The vows he'd made to her were real. Her vows had been defined and strong.

As if sensing his attention, Alina turned to meet his gaze. When she smiled shyly contentment morphed into something earthier, lustier. He'd never had the urge to swing any other woman round and then drag her into a mind-blowing kiss. Never had an impulse to sneak away at a family function for a kiss and a cuddle—maybe more. Now he stared into enticing violet eyes and imagined it all happening.

Tonight there were no shutters; her wide-eyed open expression raised the hairs on his nape. Tingled his spine. Flipped his heart. *Alina James*. The name rolled sweetly off his tongue.

'Well, Alina James, do I call for the car or do you want more dessert?'

'I'm full. It was all so delicious.'

The tip of her tongue licked her lip, as if searching for a final taste, sending a fiery jolt to his groin.

They were alone apart from the limousine driver. Ethan wrapped his arms around his bride and kissed her, slow and deep. His body responded with a sharp tug, low in his gut. She tasted sweet—pavlova-sweet. He craved more. He craved pure Alina taste.

His wife. They were legally one. She…

He was doused in a cold shower of reality. He could do nothing that might remind Alina of her first wedding night. Nothing she might regret in the morning.

He settled back holding her close, murmured, 'We'll soon be home, Mrs James,' into her ear.

Home. The word echoed in Alina's head. Her home—for as long as she chose to stay. Ethan had given the impression he meant every word of his vows. Only she knew he didn't.

'Tired, sweetheart?' The tenderness in his eyes melted her misgivings.

'Just thinking. Thank you for making tonight so wonderful, even if it's n—'

His mouth cut off the rest. Powerful and firm. Punishing. 'It's as real as any other,' he grated, tilting her face, his flashing dark eyes boring into hers. 'Don't ever forget that.'

Her body chilled, as if she'd dived into icy water. She'd offended him—the last thing she'd intended.

Tears prickled in her eyes as she struggled for words to put it right.

Suddenly she was crushed against him and kissed, with a thoroughness that left her body alive and burning.

He looked dazed when he broke away, bemused and aroused. She knew he'd see the same in her. Complete obliviousness to their surroundings.

Ethan's fingers shook as they cradled her cheek. 'Alina, darling…' He trembled as he drank her in. His reaction when she'd denied their marriage was real had astounded him. He'd endeavoured to show her how valid it was to him. Succeeded spectacularly. With a kiss like none he'd ever known.

He struggled to draw air into empty lungs, fought to clear his brain. He'd been lost in a fantasy world where the only reality was the taste of Alina on his tongue and the softness of her in his arms. Heaven.

Her stunning eyes were dark and bewildered. His stomach twisted. Bewitched by her beauty, and by her response to his kisses, he'd allowed his own ardour to override the need for restraint. Only noisy revelry out on the street as the vehicle stopped had thrown him back to reality.

He leant his forehead on hers and sucked in air scented with spring and his wife. 'I'm the one who's apologising now. Not for the kiss. Never for the kiss as long as I live. Not for anything we've shared—especially tonight. I have no right to be angry when you've complied so willingly with everything I've asked of you.'

He helped her from the car, thanked the driver and hugged her to his side as they walked to the elevator, squeezed tighter as they flew upward. When the ping announced the opening of the doors he scooped her into his arms—ignoring her protests—and stepped out.

'This is for me, sweetheart.'

Her pupils dilated, making her eyes even more alluring.

'This will be my once in a lifetime.'

He jiggled her body onto his chest as he used his key card, pushed open the door, and covered her lips with his as he carried her over the threshold. She slid her arm around his neck, her fingertips curling into his hair.

After kicking the door shut he continued the kiss, slowly letting her slide down until her feet were on the floor. Clasping her hands, he stepped back, imprinting her into his memory.

'Tonight was special in so many ways, but this

is the memory I'll keep for ever. You—so incredibly beautiful, so enticingly sweet.'

Alina watched his Adam's apple bounce as he swallowed his emotion. She'd been right in thinking their relationship might change—wrong to believe that it was a bad thing. Hormones or not, she couldn't deny she cared about Ethan James.

'You made it special, Ethan. I was… Oh, I don't know how to explain. Then you were there, and everything was right.'

'And now I have to let you go to bed.'

She heard the desire in his voice, saw it in his eyes. For a second she wondered why she wasn't pulling away and running. Then she gave her answer without any qualms.

'I'm your wife.'

She felt his tension flow out, even though their hands were their only contact. Heat flared in his eyes, quickly softening to concern.

'And much more than I deserve, Alina James. Turn around.'

He unclasped her necklace and trailed light kisses across her neck. Slipped his arms around her and drew her close, his breath teasing her earlobe.

'Go to bed, darling. While I can still let you leave. Tonight I want no regrets.'

Her cheeks burned. She'd refused to think of *that other* first night, and yet he'd understood how it might come flooding back. She'd blatantly offered herself, denying the possible—probable— consequences.

Twisting to face him, she touched her fingertips to his lips. 'I'm sorry, Ethan, I'm being selfish. I thought if you held me it wouldn't—'

'It still might. But I'll hold you in whichever bed you choose. Tonight we'll sleep. Tomorrow we'll start our honeymoon.'

She raised up onto her toes and pressed her lips to his, kept it brief.

'Thank you, Ethan.'

Her final thought as sleep overtook her was I'm Mrs Alina Paulette James…

CHAPTER FIFTEEN

ETHAN STOOD BY the lounge window, swirling his brandy in its glass, oblivious to one of Australia's most iconic views. He was reliving the emotional rollercoaster he'd ridden since the elevator doors had opened to reveal his exquisite bride.

The moment she'd seen him her stunning eyes had seemed to fill her face. She'd stopped, giving him the chance to take in every gorgeous centimetre of her. His heart had hammered; his stomach had clenched. His brain had ceased to function logically.

Her tongue-tip had flicked nervously over her tempting lips. With her bouquet held defensively over her baby bump, she'd been like a frightened animal, captured in a hunter's spotlight, unable to move. So adorable. So courageous.

He'd made no conscious decision; his movement towards her had been instinctive, as natural as breathing. Drawing her close and kissing her had eased the unaccustomed ache from being apart from her. The brightness in her eyes as they'd stood face to face, hands joined for the ceremony, had given him cause to hope.

Yet as she'd sworn, ''Till death do us part...' her fingers had lain cool in his, her voice had been calm and steady, making him wonder if she still had no intention of honouring that vow. Then she'd returned his kiss with a fervour that had made his head spin.

His cognac was failing to have its usual satisfying effect. His complete focus was on Alina.

He rinsed the glass and went to find her. She lay on her side, in *his* bed, one hand tucked under her cheek. His wife—for as long as he could persuade her to stay.

Sliding in beside her, he cradled her into his body and splayed his hand on her belly. *Alina James. Baby James.* His family. Here in his arms where he could protect them. All was right with his world.

With a deep sigh of contentment, he fell asleep.

Inching carefully out of Ethan's arms, Alina sat up, curbing the impulse to stroke his stubbled jaw. With his long dark lashes and tanned muscular body, plus a secret smile as if he were dreaming of hidden delights, he created a magazine picture that would have women lining up to buy it.

His brand-new gold ring caught her eye. She glanced down at hers, bright and shiny, a symbol of hope. She was *married*. Tendrils of the past crept into her head, were dismissed immediately. The future was unknown, not to be thought about. The now...

Her skin tingled. Lifting her head, she met Ethan's wide-awake gaze and sensual smile.

'I was looking forward to waking you with a kiss, Mrs James.' Husky. Thick.

'From your expression, whatever you were dreaming must have been better,' she teased.

A second later, she was flat on her back, drowning in dark cobalt contemplation.

'Nothing could be better than kissing my wife good morning.'

Appropriate action swiftly followed his declaration. She closed her mind, and surrendered to the ardour of his skilful lips. Everything was changing. Every day the fine line between role-playing and reality became more blurred. No longer a solitary entity, she was once again joined with someone.

'I meant to wake earlier. We have a full day in front of us, Alina.'

His rough inflections as he gulped air while trying to talk amused and thrilled her.

'Then you'd better let me go.' Teasing, half hoping he wouldn't.

He braced himself on his arms, blue eyes gleaming with suppressed delight. 'Ultrasound, then lunch. Okay?'

She nodded, not quite sure where he was going with this.

'After that my visit to tell my parents we are married will take a couple of hours. Which gives you plenty of time to pack. I've booked a holiday house in the Blue Mountains until Sunday.' He grinned like a magician who'd pulled off an amazing trick.

If an open mouth and wide eyes was the reaction he'd hoped for, he got it. Alina's heart pounded as she realised that their recent discussion on Australian tourist spots had been him info-gathering. He'd taken note of the places she'd never been to, ensuring his plans didn't clash with her memories. Another chink in her armour widened.

'Just the two of us, alone in the Blue Mountains.

Time to get to know each other better without any distractions.'

'What about work?' He'd be getting calls all day.

'All fixed. Emergencies only.'

The pavements were crowded. Alina stared through the tinted glass at people living normal lives, fiddled with her two rings. It wasn't nerves. Heck, she'd been through this procedure three times. Truth was, she was scared she might begin to care for the life inside her once she'd seen an active image on the screen. Feared she wouldn't. She wasn't sure which would be worse.

'Try to relax, Alina.' Ethan covered her restless hands with his. 'With new technology the imagery will be enhanced.'

So they'd see everything more clearly. She'd prefer vague and fuzzy.

'This was meant to be a happy time...the three of us were supposed to be together at every stage.' Her voice cracked. She bit her lip, refusing to cry.

'Now you only have me,' he remarked wryly. 'A poor substitute, but I'll do my best.'

Hearing the sorrow in his voice, she felt contrite. They were both in need of comfort.

'I wish I could talk about them without being

torn apart. About the way Leon's face lit up when he saw the blue lines, their laughter when he picked Louise up and spun her round… It hurts that their happiness only lasted a few weeks.'

'Happiness *you* gave them. For that alone I'll always be in your debt.'

He let go of her hands, hugged her so close she felt his ragged breath rumble up his chest. She thanked her lucky stars—not that there'd been much evidence that she had any—that she'd made the decision to come to him earlier rather than wait until after the birth.

A short time later Alina lay on the examination table, gripping Ethan's hand, staring at the blank monitor. He brushed his lips across her cheek.

'Our baby, Alina. An individual person.' His compelling dark eyes held her spellbound. 'Created by Leon, Louise and you. Unique in its own right.'

The technician breezed in, all smiles and goodwill. Showing soon-to-be parents images of their babies must be one of the best jobs ever.

'Hi. Alina and Ethan James, right? I'm Gary.' He grinned as he sat on the stool, checking her chart. 'Ready for some hi-tech wonder. Tuck your top up and brace yourself. Maybe one day they'll develop a lotion we can apply warm.'

He squeezed the cold gel onto her abdomen, causing her to wince and screw up her nose. Making Ethan laugh.

'Same reaction from all the dads,' Gary mused. 'Funnily enough they always refuse the offer to try it. Now, do you want to know the sex?'

'No!'

Two voices in unison. Their eyes met: hers grateful, his in accord.

'Thanks for asking,' Ethan added, his thumb moving reassuringly over her knuckles. 'We'd like to be surprised in October.'

'Lots of people still would, myself included.' He noted their refusal.

Alina watched avidly as images formed on the screen. Goosebumps peaked on her skin as she made out a moving shadowy form floating on a black background. From the dark recesses of her mind voices begged her to shut her eyes. She didn't.

The picture became clearer, the image bigger, as Gary manipulated the mouse, mouthing quiet satisfactory grunts as he worked.

'Okay, we have two arms, two legs, good proportion of head to body. Right size for fourteen weeks...' He jiggled something, the clarity increased, and then the cursor pointed to a tiny pulsating blob. 'There—can you see?—your baby's good, strong heartbeat.'

Her breath caught in her throat. Tears for her friends who would never experience this wonder filled her eyes.

A strangled gasp resonated at her side.

She swung her head and her own heartbeat stilled. Ethan's lips were parted, his eyes big and glowing with amazement. His body leant forward as far as the table permitted. His rapt expression rebooted her heartbeat into aching double time. A lifetime ago she'd seen the same wonder on another face.

She watched his Adam's apple bounce as he tried to swallow, heard his deep indrawn breath and emotional gruff tone.

'Our baby. Gives a whole new meaning to the word "daddy", doesn't it?'

'This is the moment it all becomes real,' replied the technician.

'Oh, yeah.' Ethan's smile could have lit up the city and then some. 'Thank you, Alina.'

His misty eyes chipped at her defences. His next words, whispered by her ear, tugged at her heart.

'Thank you for allowing me to be part of this incredible experience.'

She wiped a tear from his cheek and let her fingers rest on his skin. 'It's amazing, isn't it? I know the baby's there. I can see it moving. Yet I can't feel anything.'

Her brain wouldn't be forced into accepting 'our' or 'my'. That was the plan. No caring. No bonding. The right to return to her solitary life with no past, only an uncertain future. The day she'd flown to Australia she'd had no doubts it was the best possible outcome.

Since meeting Ethan certainties were becoming cloudy and convictions ambiguous. Somewhere in the clump of wool that masqueraded as her decisive mind was the niggling certainty that this was being caused more by the man who was regarding her now as if she was all the treasures he'd ever dreamed of rolled into one than by her condition.

Ethan's gaze swung from the monitor to Alina and back. He didn't know whether to holler out loud or cry. That indistinct wriggling blur was his niece or nephew—living proof that he hadn't totally lost the two people he loved most. Five weeks ago unpredictable and unbelievable. Now an almost touchable actuality.

In less than one of those rapid heartbeats he lost his heart. Utterly. Irrevocably. For ever. *Our baby.* Now he truly believed what he'd originally claimed for appearances' sake. At that instant he became a father, silently vowing to become the kind of daddy his friend would have been.

His interest in the technology vanished. He was filled with reverent awe, seeing life as it began. In six months this tiny creature would emerge as a living, breathing person. *His* child, *his* responsibility for life. He wondered how he'd ever believed he was as unemotional as his parents. His heart had swelled fit to burst.

Alina brushed away tears he hadn't realised he'd shed. Touched his cheek. A new softness shone in her beautiful eyes, curved in her smile. However deep she'd buried her maternal instincts, it wasn't enough. The natural mother he suspected her to be was going to surface, no matter how hard she fought it.

His mouth felt dry, his chest tight. His heartbeat powered up. Whether because of their baby or her it didn't matter. From this moment they really were a family. The voice in his head was telling him to somehow keep it that way.

'Okay, Mum and Dad, I've got the information I need.'

Ethan blinked as the monitor clicked off. Over already? He wanted to watch longer, see more.

'Check with the receptionist for your photos and DVD.' The technician handed Alina a box of tissues. 'Good luck. I might see you when you come in again.'

Ethan took the tissues and began to wipe off the gel, desperate to be physically involved, not wanting to come down from his euphoria. He concentrated on her stomach, absurdly self-conscious after revealing a side of him few people had ever seen.

Coward. He'd said thank you—a pathetic reward for the miracle she'd brought to him.

Throwing the tissues in the bin, he turned to meet compassionate violet eyes. A deep yearning, alien to his normal awareness, flowed through him. Along with the desire to cherish and protect as long as he lived. He shook with its intensity.

'Ethan, are you all right?'

Her fingers rested on his arm. For her a friendly gesture. For him, much more.

'Better than I've ever been.'

He smoothed her top down and helped her from the bench. Kissed her tenderly until he ran out of breath, needing her gentleness, her sweetness. *Her.*

'Let's go home, darling.'

After an early lunch Ethan drove to his parents' home alone, psyching himself up for the confrontation. He'd always been the mediator, acting as a buffer for others. Not any more. Today he was the activist.

His parents' judgemental nature along with their unachievably high standards had caused so many problems. He was convinced their agreement to Louise's marriage had been motivated only by the idea of hosting a flash high society event. It was their interference that had motivated the newlyweds to move to Barcelona. Now they'd gone he had no one else to champion. Except the quiet beauty he'd left alone in their apartment, and the grandchild he *might* inform his parents was on the way.

He walked round the house, growling in frustration. It was ridiculous that their offspring had to use the front door like guests once they'd left home, that he had to ring the bell even though they must know he'd arrived. His greeting to his father was polite, yet clipped, the reply mundane.

'This must be important, for you to take time off from work. Is it something to do with the estate?'

As expected, no welcome.

'No.'

He walked straight to the lounge. His mother sat in her chair, perfectly groomed. Just once he'd like to see her in casual clothes, with mussed-up hair. His thoughts flew to the heart-warming image of his wife in the blue chainstore outfit she'd worn at their first meeting.

'Good afternoon, Mother. I won't be stopping. I have an appointment.'

To take my bride on a honeymoon I hope will bring us even closer than we've become.

She frowned at his lack of physical greeting. He compared her barely touching air-kiss for Alina with the loving embrace he'd received from Jean when they'd met. Didn't feel the slightest guilt.

'Good afternoon, Ethan. Is there something wrong?

His father was now seated in an armchair. There was no mention of that disastrous visit, nor the fact that there'd been no further contact until yesterday morning, when he'd phoned them. They'd never deign to make a conciliatory move, and he was only here for Alina's sake.

He took the settee, placing a long envelope on the coffee table.

'I have something to tell you prior to an official announcement. If you don't approve, that's hard luck. It's a done deed.'

They both stiffened. He paused. This was for his sister, his friend. *Their baby.*

'Alina and I were married yesterday evening.'

'What?' His father sprang up.

'Sit down, Martin.'

Sophia's curt tone had its effect. He obeyed, glaring at his son. She continued, her censure radiating through the air.

'Is this some sort of warped joke because you took umbrage at our concerns over her background? I know application forms need to be lodged a month before, so...'

'It was done. We had a quiet wedding, with friends as witnesses.'

His mother went rigid, unusually lost for words. It was his father who spoke.

'Really, Ethan. We coped with immature dramas from your sister. Never expected any from *you.* You've always been practical and reasonable—'

'Maybe too much so,' Ethan cut in brusquely. 'I lost precious time with Louise and Leon because you would not accept they were meant for each other. Time I'll never get back now they're gone.'

Dismissing the protests that erupted from both of them, he leant forward, balanced his elbows on his knees and clenched his hands together.

'I love Alina.' Not a lie. It wasn't the same as being *in* love. How could he not love someone who'd given him the most priceless gift he'd ever have? 'And anyone who upsets or disrespects her will be out of my life. I don't give a damn what people think or say. Accept it or not—she's my wife, my priority.'

He waited, quite prepared to walk out. The looks they exchanged didn't faze him. He didn't care what explanation they gave their social acquaintances for his hurried secret wedding. Their society image mattered only to *them*. Tragedy had taught him that there were far more important things in life.

His mother finally found her voice. 'How are we supposed to explain this rushed event to our friends?'

All they cared about was how it would affect their image. He almost laughed out loud—couldn't remember when he'd last heard genuine amusement from either of them. Alina had a quiet sense of humour, enjoyed quirky comedies, and encouraged him to see the fun in them too.

'That's not my concern.' He flicked the envelope with his finger. 'This is a copy of the notice that will be placed in the paper on Saturday, plus a list of friends and relatives whom I will inform later this week. I would prefer you to wait until then to tell anyone else. We'll be away on our honeymoon until Sunday, so I'll only be answering urgent calls.'

'What about the Starburst chain?' His father sounded shell shocked.

'Under control.'

'I see. As usual, you've covered everything.'

He wasn't fooled by his mother's resigned tone.

'Will we see you when you return?'

He hesitated. Dared he trust them around Alina, especially as her pregnancy would soon be apparent?

'That depends on your attitude. Our baby's due in October.'

Ignoring their gasps and aggrieved expressions, he stood up.

'I'm happier right now than I have ever been in

my life, and thrilled that my wife is carrying my baby. Anyone who isn't can just stay away.'

He said goodbye soon after, breathing a sigh of relief as he went through the gates. He ought to feel guilty for the subterfuge. Instead his head was filled with Alina—her beguiling smile, the way her violet eyes revealed her emotions. Her extraordinary courage.

My wife. The simple yet profound phrase kept repeating in his brain. As he drove, singing along off-key with the radio, he felt giddy and irrationally happy. He was going home to claim another long kiss, as sweet as the one they'd shared before he left.

CHAPTER SIXTEEN

'TURN RIGHT IN four hundred metres. Clifftop Lane.'

Ethan obeyed the GPS instruction, grateful for the hassle-free drive. He pulled up in front of a white weatherboard house, switched off the engine and checked the time.

'Twelve minutes short of the two-hour estimate. You feeling okay, darling?'

'Apart from needing to stretch. This car rides much smoother than most of the vehicles I've travelled in.' She opened her door.

He was there to help before her foot touched the ground. Arching his back, he drew in a deep breath. 'Ahh…'

Alina followed suit. 'Eucalyptus. Invigorating! True Australian aroma.'

His heart sang. Could she look any more beautiful, any happier? 'Shall we take a look inside?' He jingled the keys he'd picked up on the way through Katoomba.

'Can we go for a walk first? I'd like to see the sun set on the mountains.'

They walked along the path behind the house. Through the trees they saw glimpses of brown, green and gold against a darkening blue sky, dotted with pink-tinged clouds.

'Picture-perfect.' Alina sighed, stopping to implant it into her memory.

'I agree,' Ethan replied, ignoring the scenery and embracing her from behind. He trailed soft kisses over her neck, revelling in the way she quivered with each one. Trembled himself when she twisted round, wrapped her arms around his neck and pressed her lips to his.

He inhaled the spring essence that was Alina. Fought the craving to show her how much he wanted her. His heart pounded into his ribs. And darn near exploded when her lips parted, inviting more intimate contact.

Without hesitation he accepted, loving her with his tongue, aligning their bodies with pleasurable strokes of his hands, letting her know how blatantly he was aroused. His world shrank to the two of them. It was all he needed, all he desired.

Alina arched into him, letting his heat simmer through her, returning his kiss with a passion that shook her. Her anticipation had been building since they'd arrived, diminished by the expectation of guilt. When it hadn't come, she'd pushed the boundary by kissing him.

Danger signals abated to an almost inaudible buzz. Painful consequences were a long way in the future. For the moment she was caught in the *now*. Yearning overrode everything, holding the darkness at bay.

Necessity for air broke them apart. The transparent desire in Alina's eyes told Ethan all he wanted to know.

He swung her up, cradling her close to his chest. 'Mine.' Hoarse with emotion.

'Yours…' Hot. Breathless. Murmured into the skin above his polo shirt.

He strode back to the house, king of his universe.

The sun's rays teased Alina's eyelids open. She blinked, snuggled further under the cover, trying to recapture the magic of her dream. Reached out for…

Her eyes flew open.

She was cradled by a solid wall of naked muscle, moving to a gentle rhythm. Warm breath tickled her earlobe. Firm fingers lay on her hip. A delicious glow spread from her core to every extremity at the memory of Ethan's ardent lovemaking. She turned over to look at him.

Ethan. Her husband. Her lover. Her lips curled as she recalled the tension in his muscles as he'd held his own need in check, caressing and soothing her until her barriers had finally exploded in a fiery burst of passion.

A wave of shyness engulfed her. He was a mature man who'd made love to many women. She'd only known the gentleness of first love before. Ethan had awakened the woman in her, freed her heart. But did he want it? Swearing to care for her and protect her was an abyss away from loving her.

He made a low contented sound in his throat, rolled onto his back and arched. Lazy cobalt eyes opened, widened. His lips curled in a slow, satisfied smile that held such tenderness it tugged at her heart.

'This is the perfect way to wake in the morning.'

He reached out for her, covering her mouth with his, his tongue tempting her lips to open for him. How could they not when she'd hardly recovered from the dizzy heights he'd taken her to during the night? In this big bed that she'd never forget.

'Ethan, I…' Where were coherent words when she needed them? 'Last night I…'

'Last night was more than I'd dreamt it would be…so much more than I'd fantasised.' He stroked her tousled hair, tangled his fingers through her curls. 'Promise me you won't regret what we shared. I sure as hell won't. Never. Not for a second as long as I live.'

Alina yearned to drown in the dark blue pools of his eyes, longed to share it all again now. Couldn't say the words.

Ethan ached to make love to her again, but saw the confusion in her bemused violet eyes. Knew he'd have to wait. Knew he'd have to find the right moment to tell her he wanted to make this marriage real in every way. Wanted her to always be his wife.

'Go shower.' Sometime soon he'd share one with her. 'I'll get breakfast, then we'll go sightseeing.'

She nodded, shuffled to the edge of the bed and hesitated. He smiled, loving her shyness even though she'd been married before. Was married *now*. He couldn't contain his chuckle as she shot from the bed. Paid for it as his body reacted to the sight of her running naked to the en suite. Pulling on his boxers, he headed for the kitchen, planning their day, their evening. Their night.

'Ethan!'

The panic in her voice froze his blood, sending him racing for the bathroom, his heart pumping. A heart that screeched to a halt at the sight of her huge frightened violet eyes. He dropped to his knees in front of her, hunched forward on the toilet lid, wrapped in a white towel, her arms clasping her stomach. Dragged her to his chest, fighting his own gut-wrenching fear.

'Alina, darling—tell me. What's wrong?'

She shuddered. A pain-filled cry jarred against his bare skin. 'It h-h-hurts. In my stomach—'

Her stuttering stopped with a sharp sound that cut through him.

For a second his mind went blank, refusing to process the horror her words evoked. Then it cleared. Alina needed a practical, take-action man. Lifting her as if she were delicate china, he carried her to the bed, brushing his lips across her forehead. Telling her everything would be all right. Silently cursing the fates for putting her through more torment.

Grabbing his mobile, he opened Alina's unpacked suitcase, rummaging for underwear and a dress with one hand, thumbing his phone with the other. He wrestled into the jeans and polo top he'd worn on the trip and slid on his sneakers one-handed, holding the phone to his ear with the other.

His answers to the operator's questions were clear and precise. Details could wait. Alina was frightened. His heart wrenched every time she shuddered and cried out. Their tiny baby might be in danger. He didn't dare think beyond getting them to the hospital—thankfully not too far away.

With a plan in action, he helped Alina into her clothes. He murmured reassuring phrases he'd never be able to recall, trying to ignore the resurging irrational fear gnawing at his insides. He told them both how cherished they were. He couldn't, *wouldn't* lose either of them. They were so close to becoming a family, and he'd fight like hell to keep that prospect attainable.

True to the operator's word, a medical team and trolley were waiting at the emergency entrance of the hospital. They whisked her away, leaving him to find a place to park.

Walking through the front doors, he was confronted with corridors, signs, and not a trace of Alina. Now she and their baby were in good care his composure crashed. His life, his future, was somewhere in this building and he wanted to be close to them.

He needed them. They needed him.

There'd be a path from his prowling back and forth worn into the waiting area if they didn't come for him soon. How far away was she? Had she asked for him?

He repeatedly checked his watch, matched it with the clock on the wall, tensed when anyone in hospital garb walked in.

The guilt gnawing at him now was worse than he'd felt after Louise and Leon had died. This time he'd been actively to blame. Last night when Alina had welcomed him with kisses and caresses he'd loved her with a passion that had shaken him to his core. Emotions he'd have claimed not to be any part of him had surfaced, taking them both soaring to the edge of ecstasy and tipping them over.

This was *his* fault. That book said sex was safe after the first trimester as long as there were no problems. He hadn't considered that there might be. He slammed a fist into his other palm. Prayed to all the gods that anyone believed in not to let Alina suffer another loss.

'Mr James?'

He swung round and locked eyes with a man who hardly looked old enough to be an intern.

'I'm sending your wife for an ultrasound and she's asked for you to be with her. This way.'

They fell into step and he continued. 'The physical examination shows nothing wrong. There's no bleeding, and your child's vital signs are strong.'

Ethan's brain filtered out whatever came next. Tension whooshed out of him, leaving him loose and vulnerable. *Nothing wrong. Strong vital signs.* Their baby was a fighter. It didn't lessen his culpability.

'Doctor, last night we made love. Could that have been the cause?'

'Alina told me. It might have some bearing, maybe not. Even if the ultrasound shows all's well I'd like to keep her in at least overnight, so we can monitor them both.'

'Do whatever's necessary to keep them both safe.'

Ethan sank into a chair in the private room, his eyes glued to the monitor recording their baby's heartbeat. He tried to swallow the lump in his throat as he watched that life-affirming pulse—faster than his, normal for an unborn child.

He hadn't let go of Alina's hand the whole time, needing the contact more than he needed air to breathe. His fingers caressed her knuckles. His free hand brushed strands of hair from her forehead. It tore him apart to see her so pale, so still, with a drip inserted in her wrist. He didn't know what it was—didn't care as long as it helped. Her breathing was steady; his was as erratic as leaves in a windstorm.

'If you'd like a break I can sit with her while you go for coffee.' A nurse laid a comforting hand on his shoulder.

'No, I have to be here. I have to be with them.' He wasn't going anywhere.

Ethan wasn't going anywhere. He'd even walked alongside the trolley, his hand wrapped around hers, but for the first time his warmth hadn't been able dispel Alina's icy chills. Everything had been a blur since he'd carried her from the en suite, his soft words unintelligible through the fog in her mind.

Her barricades had crashed back up with the first stab of pain, sucking her into the dark void of bereavement and despair. Resisting the impulse to cling to him, she'd lain passive in his arms as he'd carried her to the bed and the car, desperately trying to close down her nightmare.

During the ultrasound she kept her eyes closed, blanked out the technician's voice and Ethan's replies. Didn't comprehend what he said to her, only realised by the squeeze of her fingers and his kiss on her forehead that the baby was okay. For now.

Then something deep inside her shifted, shimmied through her, releasing a long-denied emotion. She gasped at the overwhelming surge of love for the tiny child fighting for survival inside her.

'Alina, does it hurt?'

The anguish in his voice focused her thoughts. She looked up, saw the furrows in his brow, the clench of his jaw, and stared into anguished eyes. Cobalt blue eyes in a captivating face that, without her realising, had become as dear to her as Colin's. She loved him—loved him *and* the baby.

No! To love was to risk everything. Mind-numbing. Terrifying. She'd fought her way back once. If she lost again she'd *never* recover.

Scrunching her eyes shut, she forced her mind to think of the remote places she'd escaped to before. Anything but him, his eyes, his touch, the way he'd loved her last night. She forced herself back to the emotionless detachment that had kept her heart safe for seven years.

Two days later Ethan took her back to the holiday house.

The next morning they returned to Sydney.

She'd done it again. Slipped away while he still slept. In the four weeks since her stay in hospital Alina had drifted into an abstract world Ethan wasn't privy to. She lay apathetic in his arms at night, rarely initiated conversation and almost never smiled. He'd built an empire with persuasion and action—now nothing he said or did helped.

He'd ensured she had time with Jean and with Dr Conlan, hoping she'd open up to one of them, or both. Giving her time and space, he hadn't pressed her, had kept their daily life as normal as possible while letting her know he'd change his schedule any time she needed him. He'd encouraged her to use her computer, knew she didn't, tried to be reassuring without crowding her.

At night he cradled her and caressed her until she fell asleep in his arms. Every day he let her know how precious she was to him in words and actions.

He was determined that she'd understand how much he cared for and wanted her, even though he made no attempt to make love to her. For her sake and their baby's.

More than anything he ached for what might have become a special part of his day: waking with Alina nestled against him, her hand over his heart, her breath soft on his chest. He longed to start each morning by kissing her awake, his heart soaring as she reacted sleepily, returning his ardour as her senses awoke.

This morning he found her in the kitchen, making herbal tea. His pulse raced even as his heart twisted at the sight of her slumped posture. He lifted her chin, dipped his head, watching for a flicker in her sorrowful eyes. The same flicker that had raised his hopes time after time, only to dash them as it quickly died.

He stepped away, ran agitated fingers through his hair. He'd been patient, willing to try anything to reach her, knowing she wasn't to blame. Today he'd run out of ideas.

'Alina, talk to me. We can work through this together, but I need to know how you feel, what you're thinking.'

She backed away, fuelling his frustration. 'I don't feel anything. Nothing.'

'Try, darling. For me. For our baby.'

She shook her head, squared her shoulders in defiance. Raised her voice. 'I can't. *I can't.*'

He bunched his fingers to prevent himself from hauling her close and kissing her hot and hard in an attempt to melt the ice that held her prisoner. Knew he was close to doing just that.

'Forget breakfast. I need space to think.' He strode to the door, grabbing his keys on the way.

His stormy departure stunned Alina, leaving her breathless, mouth gaping, fingers curled tight. She sank to the floor, leaning against the cupboard. That was the same expression she'd seen once before, when he'd walked out of their first meeting, angry, shattered.

Then she'd been unsure if she'd see him again. Now the same feeling washed over her, so much stronger. She felt desolated. Abandoned. Alone.

Wrapping her arms around her swelling stomach, she hugged herself and rocked, chest tight and body trembling. Suddenly she stilled. She wasn't alone. Her hands were cradling their baby. *Their baby.* Ethan was right: it was easy to say it once you believed.

She also believed he'd never desert Louise's child. It was his prime consideration.

He'd given his word to take care of them both. Since her stay in hospital he'd been gentle, compassionate, treating her as if she were fragile. He cuddled her close at night, whispered comforting words she hardly heard, and never attempted to make love to her.

Because he was protecting her and their baby? Because Dr Conlan had advised him not to?

She'd driven him away—maybe lost him. One night of loving might be all she'd have to remember…a magical night that…

He'd said it had been more than he'd dreamt, more than he'd fantasised. She closed her eyes and pictured his face when he kissed her, always with open eyes.

Now she recognised the love that shone in that darkening blue. Every act, every caress had been for love. For her. For their baby.

A wave of serenity washed over her. She went to the window, seeing only his smile, his quirky eyebrow rising. His cobalt blue eyes, so suspicious at first. So frustratingly angry when he'd left today because of her withdrawal, her stupidity in not sharing her fears and giving him the chance to help her.

Could he ever forgive her?

Please let him come home soon so she could tell him how much she loved him *and* their baby. She'd try to explain the mind-numbing grief, beg for his understanding and help. If he still wanted her she longed to stay, to be his wife and this baby's mother. The three of them could become a real family...

CHAPTER SEVENTEEN

TURNING LEFT AT ground level, Ethan walked aimlessly without stopping, crossing streets or turning corners depending on the traffic lights. His brain spun; his gut churned. He was the mediator, the one who found solutions. Why not for Alina? He'd broken her barriers down before—now he seemed to be the reason they'd been rebuilt.

He sidestepped a toddler, squirming in his mother's grip, quirked a smile at them both. Hopefully that was his future—an active, adventurous child with Louise and Leon's DNA. Their love of life, their loyalty, their… His throat tightened. Would there be anything of Alina? How could there not be when she'd nourished and cocooned their baby for nine months?

A red light. He swung left. Ahead lay Circular Quay and the Manly Ferry.

Alina's eyes had sparkled that day; her smile had enthralled him. He'd loved her sweet response to his kiss. Loved her… *Loved her.*

He stopped short, barely registering the stroller slamming into the back of his leg or the young father's apology.

'Not your fault, mate. I stopped.'

And he'd stopped being an idiot. He moved over to the building, his body trembling as he acknowledged how much of one he'd been. That original tightening in his gut, his complete trust in her from the start and the primal urge to protect her... His desire to know her would have been as strong whenever, *however* he'd met her.

Alina had captured his heart from the moment he'd stood in that doorway. He hadn't realised it because he hadn't believed he was capable of the feeling. For weeks he'd been following a nightly ritual in secret, not comprehending he'd truly meant it for both of them. If he'd let himself believe he might have prevented the rebuilding of her barricades.

He began to run—back to the apartment, back to claim her for his own. Back to offer her his love and life.

Opening and then closing the door silently, he moved forward, muscles tense, pulse racing. Heart praying.

Alina stood by the window, staring out. It was

an echo of their first meeting, only this time he rejoiced in the gloriously familiar gut-clench.

Alina stroked her stomach, whispered words of encouragement, letting their baby know everything was going to be all right.

'Your daddy's temper flares quickly…cools almost as fast. He'll ponder the problem, think out a solution. Come home to take action.'

The back of her neck tingled.

'Alina?'

She turned, her heart flipping at his voice. Cobalt blue eyes set in impassive features scanned hers with the deep intensity she knew so well. His muscles were taut, as if prepared to ward off a devastating blow. His lips twitched.

Her mouth dried. Chills ran down her spine. She couldn't move.

He came towards her. His arms swung out, fingers spread. 'I can't go on like this.'

She froze. He couldn't mean it. He couldn't leave her. Or send her away. Her legs felt like jelly and yet they refused to buckle.

Her brain screamed. *Tell him you want to stay. Tell him you love him.*

The words wouldn't come.

One more step brought him close enough to caress her baby bump. He didn't.

'Can you imagine what it's like, waiting for you to fall asleep every night before I can tell you how much I love you?'

Grated out as if in protest.

Heat raced through her veins. Her legs crumpled. Ethan caught her, crushing her to his chest.

'You *do* that?'

He'd been saying he loved her. *He did love her.* Her arms wrapped around his neck, holding fast.

'Every night for weeks. I believed I was incapable of loving the way Leon and Louise did, so I told myself it was for our baby. Persuaded myself the physical attraction was because you were so beautiful, so sweet and courageous.'

His eyes sparkled. His hands soothed her. His brilliant smile was for her alone.

'I love you, Alina James. Probably from the moment I saw you. Recognising it took my head longer than my heart. Stay with us. I swear—'

'I love *you*, Ethan James. There's nowhere else I want to be.'

Ethan's lips sought hers tenderly, lovingly, savouring the taste of her, becoming more fervent as she responded in kind. He heard a low groan of desire, wished it were hers. Knew it came from him.

Breaking the kiss, he scooped her up, settling on the settee with her in his lap, her head on his shoulder, his hand splayed over her growing baby bump.

'I'm sorry for not trusting you to help me, Ethan. I've been so scared of losing you, losing you both. So fearful of getting trapped in the darkness again, being alone with no way out this time. You saved me and I pushed you away.'

'We're together now, and nothing's—'

His heart lurched as she suddenly sat up, eyes vivid and wide, a delighted smile lighting up her face.

'Our baby *moved*! Like a tiny ripple. Ethan, our baby's letting us know we're not alone.'

He kissed her softly, reverently. 'I promise you'll never be alone again, my love.'

September thirtieth.
Baby active.
Kept Alina up most of the night.

Ethan closed the diary and stretched. Alina was resting in the lounge, at his insistence, after rising early, claiming she couldn't get comfortable in bed.

He was just about to check if she wanted anything, tell her he'd work from home today, when she waddled in.

Her concerned expression had him on his feet in an instant.

'Do you need something, darling?'

'I didn't tell you earlier—thought it might be a false alarm.'

His body hit full alert in a heartbeat. He crossed the room, clasped her arms and pinned her with a warning glare.

'The contractions started before dawn. I've been timing them and—'

'Don't say it.' If it was voiced out loud it might happen. 'We've got three weeks to go. Must be a Braxton-Thick false alarm thing.'

Please let it be.

She gave him an indulgent smile. 'Braxton-*Hicks*—and that's why I waited until I was sure. I finished packing the bag, in case, then phoned Dr Conlan. She said she'll meet us at the hospital and to drive carefully.'

'No ambulance? No paramedics, trained in case the baby comes en route?'

'We have plenty of time, Ethan. I promise. The hire car's on its way.'

He strode from the room. Came back frowning.

'We need to…um…*hell*!' His mind was a fuzz-ball.

The hospital bag. He walked to the door, pivoted at the musical sound he normally loved to hear. His gorgeous wife was laughing at his indecision—a moment after telling him she was in premature labour.

He did the only thing a man could do in the circumstances: pulled her close to stop her mirth with his mouth. A breathless eternity later he lifted his head. It was time to man up. Or daddy up. He knelt to kiss her stomach, then splayed both hands there.

'Okay, bub, your timing's out, but you're in charge. Unless you want to reconsider and stay where you are, nice and cosy for another three or four weeks.'

His response was a firm kick. With a wry grin he straightened up.

'I guess we're gonna have a baby, Mrs James. You keep timing the contractions. I'll get the bag.'

'You'll have to call your mother on the way.'

His features hardened. 'Why the hell would I do that?'

In five months he'd only occasionally seen them socially, phoned them when necessary. Refused to give them any chance of upsetting Alina.

'Jean and I bumped into her at a baby shop last week. We talked for a few minutes, then arranged to have lunch today. I was going to tell you how it went tonight.'

'My mother was in a *baby shop*?' An unbelievable event. She ordered gifts online from exclusive stores.

His features softened and he drew Alina as close as their baby allowed.

'You agreed to meet her after the way they treated you? You are a very special lady, Alina James, and I'm a very lucky man.'

Dr Conlan was waiting for them. As Alina was wheeled away Ethan caught her arm.

'It's too soon. You said late October.'

She patted his hand and smiled. 'Babies don't always follow our planning chart, Ethan. This one's decided today's its birthday, whether we're ready or not.'

He wasn't. This was his woman. Their baby. He

desperately wanted to take her home, where he could keep them both safe until the due date.

'Can't you delay it? At least until our baby's bigger?'

'Too late for that. Looks like your child's made an executive decision. Welcome to fatherhood, with all its unpredictability.'

It was happening. Louise's baby. Louise who'd hated being late for anything, who had always been early, eager to savour the first moment, the overture. His little miracle was about to be born.

Adrenaline pumped through his veins. It was like that exultant moment in a business deal when he knew he was on the cusp of victory. Only a thousand times better.

It wasn't the exclusive birthing suite he'd booked. Didn't matter. They were in the safest place possible. Dr Conlan was there, there were paediatric specialists within call. He could see the special incubator, positioned discreetly by the wall.

He rubbed Alina's back and encouraged her to puff and blow. Wiped the sweat from her brow, kissed her and repeatedly told her how much he loved her. He wished he could take the pain for her, and didn't flinch when her nails dug into his hand.

'Okay, Daddy, let me take over here.'

The nurse was there, nudging him aside. He growled. 'No.'

This was *his* place. *His* prerogative.

'Go help deliver your baby.'

Deliver? Him? He looked at Alina, who nodded. 'Go.'

Her reassuring smile filled his heart to bursting point.

An urgent, 'Come on, Ethan!' had him scrambling to the doctor's side.

He obeyed instructions, his eyes totally focused on the thick thatch of damp dark hair emerging. A whoosh of movement and suddenly his arms were full of a squirming, slippery, wrinkled creature. He intuitively hugged the red-faced newborn to his pounding heart, fascinated by the petite button nose and bow lips.

When a delightful squeak became a distinctive howl of objection he blinked away his tears of joy. They had a daughter. He was a fair dinkum father.

'Hi, bub. We've been waiting for you.'

To his amazement, as if soothed by his voice, her crying was tempered to a whimper and the cutest hiccup. He gazed into unfocused cobalt blue eyes, a reminder of Louise, then looked at Alina, who lay with her head back, face pale and eyes closed. And loved her even more.

He watched impatiently as this miniature of his sister was weighed and checked, exulted when her fingers wrapped around the one he used to touch her palm lightly. Scowled when she gave a tiny mew as they took a blood sample from her heel.

With the doctor's all-clear he carried their baby to the woman he adored beyond reason. His hopes soared as her eyes opened to reveal misty love-filled violet. As he gently lowered their little girl into her arms he held his breath, praying this little angel would finally erase the last vestige of her grief.

'We have a little girl, my darling. A beautiful daughter.' He said it proudly, aloud for the world to hear. His next whispered words were for her alone. 'As beautiful as her mothers. *Both* of them.'

Still cradling his daughter's head, he wrapped his arm around his wife. He believed his emotions had peaked until her finger softly caressed the tiny cheek, and they zoomed even higher. His heart threatened to burst through his chest as she pressed her lips to the ruddy pink forehead. She gazed down in wonder, her lips curled into the most beautiful smile he'd ever seen.

When she looked at him, her eyes shone like diamonds. 'We have a daughter, Ethan. I love you both so much,' she said huskily.

Her words thrilled him. Her kiss echoed her spoken words.

Alina had welcomed his tender caresses, his declarations of affection as he'd tried to ease her pain. Had seen his disconcertion at the nurse's attempt to take over. She'd always treasure the memory of his startled expression when their baby had slid into his hands, quickly replaced by one of wondrous awe as he tenderly gathered the precious bundle to his chest. She saw a tiny fist waving in protest and felt her breasts respond to the plaintive cry.

Her heart had blipped when he'd nestled the baby into her arms. Blipped and then beaten steady and strong as she saw dark hair, cobalt blue eyes, bow lips and long fingers: the perfect blend of her natural parents. As she'd touched the soft rosy cheek the last trace of anguish had faded, leaving only the gentler sorrow for what might have been.

She choked up at the sight of Ethan's hand cradling their daughter's head—protective, loving. The way he'd cradled *her* from the start. With tenderness and patience he'd demolished her defences, allowing her to recall the good memories without pain, allowing her to love again.

She kissed their daughter's brow and guided her searching mouth to her breast. Rejoiced at the ecstasy of this unique moment of bonding. *Their daughter.* How wonderful it sounded now.

Gazing at her husband she wondered if a heart could burst with joy. She stretched her neck to kiss him, luxuriating in the knowledge that he was hers. Basking in the glow from his darkening cobalt eyes.

'Louisa.' He stroked their daughter's hair. 'A priceless gift. Very much wanted and loved.'

'Louisa Leona James,' she countered. 'A mother has naming rights too.'

* * * * *

MILLS & BOON®
Large Print – November 2016

Di Sione's Innocent Conquest
Carol Marinelli

A Virgin for Vasquez
Cathy Williams

The Billionaire's Ruthless Affair
Miranda Lee

Master of Her Innocence
Chantelle Shaw

Moretti's Marriage Command
Kate Hewitt

The Flaw in Raffaele's Revenge
Annie West

Bought by Her Italian Boss
Dani Collins

Wedded for His Royal Duty
Susan Meier

His Cinderella Heiress
Marion Lennox

The Bridesmaid's Baby Bump
Kandy Shepherd

Bound by the Unborn Baby
Bella Bucannon

MILLS & BOON®
Large Print – December 2016

The Di Sione Secret Baby
Maya Blake

Carides's Forgotten Wife
Maisey Yates

The Playboy's Ruthless Pursuit
Miranda Lee

His Mistress for a Week
Melanie Milburne

Crowned for the Prince's Heir
Sharon Kendrick

In the Sheikh's Service
Susan Stephens

Marrying Her Royal Enemy
Jennifer Hayward

An Unlikely Bride for the Billionaire
Michelle Douglas

Falling for the Secret Millionaire
Kate Hardy

The Forbidden Prince
Alison Roberts

The Best Man's Guarded Heart
Katrina Cudmore

MILLS & BOON®

Why shop at millsandboon.co.uk?

Each year, thousands of romance readers find their perfect read at millsandboon.co.uk. That's because we're passionate about bringing you the very best romantic fiction. Here are some of the advantages of shopping at www.millsandboon.co.uk:

* **Get new books first**—you'll be able to buy your favourite books one month before they hit the shops

* **Get exclusive discounts**—you'll also be able to buy our specially created monthly collections, with up to 50% off the RRP

* **Find your favourite authors**—latest news, interviews and new releases for all your favourite authors and series on our website, plus ideas for what to try next

* **Join in**—once you've bought your favourite books, don't forget to register with us to rate, review and join in the discussions

Visit **www.millsandboon.co.uk**
for all this and more today!